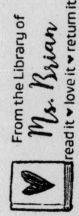

THE HIDDEN WORLD OF
Changers

No. 8: The Changer War

by H. K. Varian

Simon Spotlight

New York London Toronto Sydney New Delhi

This book is a work of fiction. Any references to historical events, real people, or real places are used fictitiously. Other names, characters, places, and events are products of the author's imagination, and any resemblance to actual events or places or persons, living or dead, is entirely coincidental.

SIMON SPOTLIGHT

An imprint of Simon & Schuster Children's Publishing Division
1230 Avenue of the Americas, New York, New York 10020
This Simon Spotlight paperback edition October 2017
Copyright © 2017 by Simon & Schuster, Inc.
Text by Laurie Calkhoven
Illustrations by Tony Foti
All rights reserved, including the right of reproduction in whole or in part in any form.
SIMON SPOTLIGHT and colophon are registered trademarks of Simon & Schuster, Inc.
For information about special discounts for bulk purchases, please contact Simon & Schuster
Special Sales at 1-866-506-1949 or business@simonandschuster.com.
Designed by Nick Sciacca
The text of this book was set in Celestia Antiqua.
Manufactured in the United States of America 0917 OFF
10 9 8 7 6 5 4 3 2 1
ISBN 978-1-5344-0146-4 (hc)
ISBN 978-1-5344-0145-7 (pbk)
ISBN 978-1-5344-0147-1 (eBook)
Library of Congress Catalog Card Number 2017952998

Selkie

Originating from the shores of Ireland and Scotland, selkies are Changers who can transform into a seal with the help of their selkie cloaks. Selkies are born with their cloaks, and as they age, the cloak ages with them. As such, selkies usually feel an intense bond with their cloak and will protect it at all costs.

Though selkies cannot transform without their cloaks, they are still one of the most powerful kinds of Changers due to their innate connection to magic. Selkie magic is manifested through the selkie songs, which can control the tide, summon storms, enchant objects, and even destroy another being's magic.

Because selkie songs are sung in a magical language, they cannot be written down or otherwise captured. The only way for a selkie youngling to learn a song is to be taught directly by another selkie.

PROLOGUE

Fiona Murphy had just returned home from a long, exhausting day in New York City. Perhaps the average girl would have been excited to visit New York City, but Fiona was hardly the "average girl."

Fiona was a *selkie*, a magical shape-shifting Changer. Up until her first day of seventh grade at Willow Cove Middle School, Fiona thought *selkies* were simply mythological creatures. Then everything changed. She learned that she was a member of a small and very secret tribe of *selkies*, and with the help of her *selkie* cloak, she could transform into a seal and rule the ocean.

Fiona often felt like she had two lives—one on land, one at sea.

As she often did, Fiona looked over the cliff's edge toward the ocean. It was a view she never tired of. Tonight the sun was a fiery ball reflecting on the waves, ranging from a deep crimson to a coppery red.

It's been too long since I've been in those waves, Fiona thought. But after all she'd just been through in New York City, when would she have time to go for a swim again?

Just as Fiona was thinking this, she caught sight of something familiar—a tuft of red hair, just over by the sea. A passerby might have missed it, but not Fiona.

"Mom," Fiona said breathlessly.

A year ago Fiona would have never believed that her mom would be waiting for her by the sea cliffs. For a long time Fiona had believed her mother was dead. But her mother was, in fact, not dead. She was Queen Leana of the *selkies.* She had to live away from her daughter until Fiona was old enough to know the truth.

Fiona's mother sauntered up to her and embraced her daughter in a warm hug.

"Fiona," her mother said. Her voice was calm and

relaxed, but Fiona could detect a slight panic in her mother's eyes. "Thank moonlight you are all right. So much has happened."

Fiona started to feel guilty. She'd only gone to New York to help a friend; she hadn't meant to worry her mother. She bit her lip.

"I'm sorry—" she started to say.

But it seemed Fiona's mother was worried about something else entirely.

"I'm afraid I have some troubling news," her mother said. "The *selkies* have learned that you've been foretold as one of the new First Four."

Fiona gasped. Her mind whirled with what-ifs. Through her mother, Fiona was *selkie* royalty. But the *selkies*' discovery of her role in the larger Changer world could spell disaster.

Fiona, along with her three friends—Mack Kimura, Darren Smith, and Gabriella Rivera—were foretold by an ancient prophecy to be the next leaders of the Changer world, the next First Four. Darren was an *impundulu*, a fearsome bird from southern Africa that could shoot lightning bolts from his razor-sharp talons and create violent storms. Gabriella was a *nahual*, a jaguar with yellow eyes, sleek jet-black fur, and the ability to spirit-walk in other people's minds. And Makoto—Mack—was a *kitsune*, a powerful white fox with paws that blazed with fire. He had the ability to fly and to borrow other Changers' powers, just like his *kitsune* grandfather, who helped train them.

In their training, Fiona had learned that long ago, Changers lived openly alongside humans. In fact, Changers did their best to protect humans from the world's dark forces. But the concept of real magic was too much for human brains to grasp. Thousands of years ago humans came to believe that Changers wanted to destroy them.

Fear is a strange thing. And fear—as fear does—made the humans act in strange, desperate ways. The Changers were forced to create a hidden world. They were still devoted to protecting humans from evil, but now they did so in secret—and from a distance.

Fiona, Darren, Mack, and Gabriella learned all of this in their training at the hands of the First Four, the current leaders of all Changer-kind.

Akira Kimura, Mack's grandfather, steered Fiona and

her friends in the discovery and control of their new powers. Dorina Therian, a werewolf, was the kids' primary coach in their secretly enchanted gym at Willow Cove Middle School. Yara Moreno (an *encantado*, or dolphin Changer) and Sefu Badawi (a *bultungin*, or hyena Changer) stepped in to help every now and then.

From the moment Fiona first put on her *selkie* cloak and dove into the ocean waves, she felt more like herself than ever before. The rhythm and pulse of the tides were as natural to her as breathing. It was almost like ... almost like she was *complete*.

But it was a world of deep divisions. The *selkie* faction, for instance, had a long-standing mistrust of the Changer nation. Fiona often felt torn between two *more* worlds, in addition to her human one—her mother's *selkie* world and that of the Changer nation. Especially because, thanks to the prophecy and her lineage, Fiona was due to inherit both.

Bringing those two worlds together became even trickier when a new dark force came into play. An evil *kitsune* named Sakura Hiyamoto, or the Shadow Fox, had built an army to rise against the Changer nation. Sakura wanted control of everything—the magical *and* the nonmagical—and she was ready to go to war to get it.

What's more, the Shadow Fox was a memory eater. She could consume whatever memories she wanted, insert false memories, and absorb that Changer's powers. A former student of Mr. Kimura's, she had left him so that she could delve into dark magic. Then Sakura turned on her former master, though Fiona didn't know why.

Sakura had long been underground, watching and waiting to take her revenge. But recently she had come out of hiding to amass her army—and her first target was Mack.

Mack—Fiona's friend. Mack—who was supposed to join them as the new First Four. Mack—who enjoyed making goofy faces and reading comic books.

Sakura had poisoned good, kind Mack's mind with dark magic and lured him in with promises of power. She replaced his memories of happiness and hope with those of anger and despair. Once that was complete, Mack was her pawn. He turned his back on the Changer nation and joined Sakura's dark forces.

But before they could rescue Mack, the First Four

had to make sure Fiona, Gabriella, and Darren were safe; they knew the three younglings would be the next targets. Sakura would want the complete set. She was a collector, of sorts—of powerful Changers and their abilities—and wanted them in her army. Thankfully, Fiona was protected from Sakura's mind control with her powerful *selkie* Queen's Song, and Gabriella was protected by ancient Aztec magic in the form of the Ring of Tezcatlipoca. But Darren had no such shield. That's why the group had traveled to New York City: to lift an ancient curse and to find protection for him.

Before they could do that, however, Sakura's army had mounted a surprise attack. Many had been injured, but in the end the First Four and their followers prevailed—and one *very* good thing had come out of the battle. Gabriella had spirit-walked into Mack's mind and healed the pain that Sakura had inflicted. Their friend was himself again.

Gabriella had wanted Mack to come back home to Willow Cove with them, but Mack made a brave sacrifice instead. He chose to stay with Sakura as an agent for the First Four. Mack had mastered illusion magic and believed he could mask his true self from the evil master. His plan was to feed crucial inside information to the First Four, which could be the key to victory. Fiona worried about him but knew she had to focus on her own mission too.

With war looming, Fiona and her mother had hoped the *selkies* would support the First Four. But it was a matter that required a gentle touch. Gaining that support required delicate and ongoing negotiations. Mother and daughter—queen and princess—had agreed that delicacy was only possible if Fiona's role as a member of the next First Four remain undisclosed.

But now those careful efforts had been ruined by the revelation of Fiona's secret.

Fiona was very right to be alarmed.

"The *selkies* are deeply divided about how to proceed," Fiona's mother said. "Many refuse to trust my leadership on this issue."

"How did they find out?" Fiona asked. "We've been so careful."

"I don't know," her mother answered. "There are some *selkies* who are sympathetic to Sakura's cause."

This made Fiona's stomach turn.

"Are *any selkies* on our side?" she asked.

"Some are," her mother answered. "There are those who feel comforted by the idea of a *selkie* as part of the next First Four, that leadership of the Changers will be returned to the *selkies* at last."

"But?" Fiona asked.

"But there is another *selkie* group, one that is actively undermining that belief. They're even calling into question my right to rule. They say that because I've known about the prophecy and kept it secret, that you and I are puppets of the First Four."

"But that's not true," Fiona said, her voice fading into a whisper. The word "puppet" felt like a wound to her heart. She had worked so hard to straddle those two realms, to learn everything she could about both the *selkies* and the larger Changer world. She had fought battles against evil forces and tried to get to know the needs of the various factions around her. She was *good*. She knew that. Why were people against her, still?

I'm exhausted, she thought. *All that effort, and now it's being met with lies and mistrust. It's not fair!*

"Of course it isn't true," her mother said. "You're nobody's puppet, nor am I. But this group is using that fear to try to convince the *selkies* that you're not really one of us—and that I'm not either."

Fiona took a deep breath and shook off her despair. *I've worked too hard to give up now,* she thought. Then she thought of Mack, who was *behind enemy lines*. Surely Mack had the hardest job of all. Suddenly, she didn't feel so bad for herself.

"What should we do?" she asked. "How can we make things better?"

"We must heal this division within the *selkie* faction before things get any worse. We don't need two wars on our hands," her mother said.

Fiona gasped. "*Two* wars? Do you mean the *selkies* would go to war with each other? A civil war?"

"I hope it won't go that far, but we must be sure it doesn't," her mother said. "So I've come up with a plan. You need to be more visible on the *selkie* isles. We'll move all your lessons there so the *selkies* learn you are loyal to our kind."

Fiona was about to object. The *selkies*' territory was a

half day's swim from Willow Cove. *What if I'm needed in a battle with Sakura?* she worried.

"I know you want to stick close to the First Four," her mother said, as if reading her mind. "But your distance from the *selkie* isles is one of the biggest reasons why the *selkie*s question your loyalty. You *must* strike up a friendship with some of the other youngling *selkie*s and attend the next few council meetings. Let our people see that you're interested and trustworthy. It'll make all the difference. We're just a proud group—we don't want to be run by outsiders. I know they will come to love you as I love you."

Fiona bit her lip, not sure how to respond. Darren, Gabriella, and Mack needed her. And what would her father do? He could barely boil pasta for himself! She knew her mother wouldn't ask her lightly to leave everyone, but so far her relationship with the other *selkie*s hadn't exactly been rosy. Some *selkie*s had actually made fun of her in a council meeting; others ignored her entirely.

But then another thought occurred to her. *If I really am going to be a leader one day, then I must try to unite the* selkies *with one another and perhaps with the Changer nation, too.*

Fiona was about to agree to the journey when her mother added a condition.

"As you can understand, this situation is delicate and dire," her mother said. "The selkies need to trust you completely. As it is such, you cannot share where you're going with your friends or with the First Four."

More secrets?

Fiona was apt to protest—surely she had to tell the First Four where she was going. Yes, she'd be with her mother, but—but—

Fiona lost track of her thoughts. Out of the corner of her eye, way into town, she spotted a massive lightning storm forming in the distance. A loud *crack* could be heard from overhead. Fiona looked out. Her jaw dropped. This wasn't normal, everyday lightning. This was magic lightning. And she knew where that lightning was coming from, too—it was in the direction of Darren's house.

Something's wrong, Fiona thought. *Darren wouldn't create a storm like that. Not unless he was in danger . . .*

"Fiona?" Queen Leana asked, staring at her daughter. "Fiona, do you understand me?"

Fiona took another glance at the lightning storm. It was growing stronger and stronger. She had no choice.

"I'm sorry, Mom, I really am," she said. "But I—I have to go."

Chapter 1
THE LIGHTNING

Darren stood in the entrance to his family room, watching lightning zigzag up and down his older brother Ray's arms. It was impossible, almost, that his brother could suddenly wield lightning—Darren had thought he was the only *impundulu* in the family—but it was happening nonetheless.

"Darren, stay back!" Ray yelled.

Darren could see the fear in his brother's eyes. The same fear Darren had experienced when he first came into his powers. He had no idea what was happening and, like Ray, had no control over this bizarre new power.

Darren drew his hands together and called on his own powers to create a ball of counterelectricity. Then he moved his hands apart to make a circle, forming a protective force field around the two of them. It was a success! Even though lightning still emanated from Ray's fingertips, he could no longer damage anything—or, more importantly, *anyone*.

Could it be? Darren thought. His mind was racing. Was the curse he'd meant to break in New York City lifted? If his brother suddenly had lightning powers, surely that meant the curse was lifted, that Darren's Changer bloodline was coming into their powers again, that Ray was an *impundulu* too—

And if Ray was an *impundulu*, the curse *had* to have been lifted. The Spider's Curse—which Darren had recently learned was pressed upon his family generations ago—made sure that no *impundulus* in their bloodline came to power. Somehow, Darren's powers managed to emerge, anyway.

In ancient times a bitter conflict had erupted between the spider Changers, the *anansi*, and the *impundulus* for control of a strategic region in Southwest

Africa. During the conflict the *anansi* had cursed many *impundulus* with a powerful poison contained in their bite. The curse was passed down from generation to generation and prevented all but the most powerful *impundulus* from being able to transform and discover their Changer gifts.

Darren was one of those powerful *impundulus*, but he had no other family members who were Changers. No one to help guide him in those difficult and confusing early days.

Even worse, because of that ancient curse, Darren was also unable to benefit from a protection spell that would keep him safe from Sakura's mind control. So he and the others had flown to New York City by *tengu*, a bird that commanded the wind and could transport anyone anywhere in the blink of an eye, to meet the descendant of the *anansi* who had cursed his ancestor. If the *anansi* agreed to forgive his bloodline, Darren had believed he could be protected from Sakura and her forces with an ancient spell.

Unfortunately, although Esi Akosua, the young *anansi* in question, was willing to forgive Darren, she didn't believe that would change anything for him. She had offered forgiveness to other *impundulus* her ancestors had bitten, yet the curse had remained in place.

Darren tried to think back. Had Esi forgiven him in some different way? Perhaps the fact that they hid from Sakura together made her really *mean* the forgiveness. That could certainly explain everything!

While things were coming clear for Darren, Ray was still mystified.

Ray stared at his little brother openmouthed. Darren was wielding the same kind of electrical power that was exploding from his own fingertips, and doing a much better job of it.

"You—you can—*what*?" Ray stammered.

"Er, you might want to calm down," Darren said. But Ray didn't calm down. The lightning in Ray's palms became more unstable. "Ray, you have to calm down or it won't stop."

"'Calm down'?" Ray yelled. "What do you mean calm down? There's *lightning* running up and down my arms. I can't calm down! What's happening?"

How many times had Darren imagined this

conversation? Wished that his older brother were an *impundulu* too? That he had someone to share this new and exciting power with? But in every one of those scenarios, Ray was helping *him* out, not the other way around. Darren wasn't sure what to say. He took a deep breath.

"You're an *impundulu*—a magical shape-shifting bird—and so am I."

Ray shook his head. "You're hallucinating. We must both be hallucinating."

"No, we're Changers," Darren said. He started to ramble. "I found out on the first day of school. It runs in families, and I thought I was the only one in our family, but then I found out there was a curse that blocked your powers, I guess, and Esi said it wouldn't work, but it did, and now you're one of us, and . . ."

Darren stopped and took a deep breath, but Ray didn't look any less scared and confused than he had a minute ago. There were still sparks crackling from the tips of his fingers.

"What's an Esi? What are you talking about?" Ray demanded.

I'm no good at explaining this, Darren thought. He had

so longed to share this new world with a family member, especially Ray. He had just never thought about having to be the one to explain it all.

I need to get in touch with Ms. Therian. If anyone knows how to explain this—and how to keep Ray in check—it's her, he thought.

Darren was about to call Ms. Therian when the front door slammed open.

Please don't be Mom, he thought over and over again. He didn't want to explain to his mom why her kids were suddenly enveloped in a lightning storm.

"Darren? Darren?" came a voice.

Darren recognized that voice. Thankfully, it wasn't his mom at all—it was Fiona!

For a brief second Darren was happy to hear her, but that was soon replaced with a new worry. *I don't know if I can hold the force field much longer,* Darren worried. *Fiona could accidentally get hurt.*

"Fiona!" Darren shouted back. "It's not safe. Call Ms. Therian."

"Fiona?" Ray repeated. "Your friend from school? Oh, don't tell me she's an *impun*—"

Ray's question was cut off by Fiona herself, soaking wet from the storm that raged over their house. But if she was bothered by the rain, she didn't show it. She used some of the rain droplets to weave a water shield around herself and took a look at Ray.

"Is Ray . . . ?" Fiona asked.

"Yes," Darren said.

"So the curse is . . ."

"Broken."

There was a beat of silence. Then Fiona's face brightened.

"Professor Zwane can work the protection spell now, Darren," she said earnestly. "You'll be protected from Sakura!"

"Yes, that's great," Darren said, "but right now we need to get Ms. Therian. Ray needs her help."

Fiona dropped her water shield and pulled out her cell phone. She dialed Mrs. Therian, but there was no answer. Then she dialed again. Still no answer.

"She's always by her phone," Fiona said. "Where could she be?"

An exhausted Darren dropped his guard for a second,

and that was all it took. Ray's powers were too new and unwieldy to control. A stray bolt of lightning burst from Ray's fingertips and zipped quickly past Darren—right to Fiona.

"Ack!" Fiona screamed.

It all happened in an instant.

Fire. Something smelled like fire. The room was covered in yellow light and then darkened into black. For a brief pause no lightning emanated from Ray. It was like the world froze.

"Fiona!" Darren yelled.

Was she hurt? Darren could barely see her—all he could *smell* was ash. Like something—or rather, some*one*—had just been burned. His stomach turned and he feared the worst.

Thankfully, he heard Fiona's voice.

"I'm . . . okay," Fiona replied breathlessly.

Whew. Fiona was already working on putting out the fire with water when Darren noticed what Ray had hit. It was Fiona's hair! Fiona's hair was completely buzzed on one side. For a moment he was scared, but then he couldn't help but think it looked, well, *cool*.

But there was more where that came from. Lightning ping-ponged from the wall to the ceiling and back again, all at the speed of—well, light.

"I'm sorry! I'm so sorry!" Ray kept yelling, doing his best to cover up his hands, but the lightning just wouldn't stop. Instead, with each "sorry," another jolt came bursting out.

Fiona ducked into the hall to try calling Ms. Therian again while Darren worked on building a new—and hopefully, more durable—force field. The smell of singed hair filled Darren's nostrils.

He remembered the time he almost killed Fiona in the ancillary gym where they had their Changer training. He had shot a lightning arrow that missed its mark, shattered an overhead light, and nearly fell into the saltwater pool where Fiona was training. It missed by less than an inch—and Darren felt *terrible*.

Thankfully, he'd had Ms. Therian's help then. Darren knew he needed her help again now, more than anything.

Fiona kept calling and calling, but there was no response. It was so unlike Ms. Therian. Fiona tried a few other numbers, but nothing seemed to work.

Darren didn't know what was going on.

Where are you, Ms. Therian? Darren wondered. *We need you.*

Chapter 2
BEHIND ENEMY LINES

Mack was engaged in another battle. He was exhausted. Fighting with Sakura meant fighting many battles, *many* times a day, but he couldn't blow his cover; he had to tough it out. His role as a double agent was too important. Just as he was about to attack a *mo'o*, Mack saw a flash of lightning cross the sky, illuminating the battle going on all around him. He assumed it was created by an *impundulu* because the sky was otherwise clear, but Mack was so tired and confused that he couldn't entirely be sure.

Sakura's forces had barely limped back from their last battle in New York City when the master (as Sakura preferred they call her) sent them out again. Sakura was enraged with her army on two fronts. Not only had they failed to capture any members of the First Four, they had failed to secure one of the Changers most powerful relics: Circe's Diadem. The diadem was able to awaken magical potential sleeping inside nonmagical humans, and Sakura intended to use it to help build her army. Unfortunately for her, it remained safely in the hands of Esi Akosua and the *anansi*, who, for the most part, aligned themselves with the Changer Nation.

Mack and the others had just reached their own base and begun to heal their wounds when Sakura ordered them to this remote forest in the hopes that other Changer relics were hidden here. Mack wasn't even sure in what part of the world they were, but someone had obviously tipped off supporters of the First Four. They were ready and waiting to do battle. Ms. Therian and Sefu were commanding them. Mack was relieved to not see his grandfather or any of his Willow Cove friends. Now that he was back to being himself, the idea of battling against people he cared so much about was challenging. He'd done everything possible to avoid hurting Ms. Therian and Sefu already.

An *aatxe*, or bull Changer, was charging toward him, its powerful horns ready to cut him in two. Mack somersaulted out of its way and cast a fire arrow at the assailant. It was an arrow intended to miss, not to hit, but he had to make it menacing all the same. Working as a double agent for the First Four was proving to be trickier than Mack originally thought it would be. It was much less like a comic book and much more frightening.

Mack could see that this battle was going sour for Sakura's forces, just like the last one. They had lost too many of their veteran soldiers. The new recruits were weak and easily frightened. Although grateful for this, he dreaded to think of the Shadow Fox's fury after they lost another battle.

Will she blame me? Mack wondered. *I have to make her think I'm still her apprentice, that I still worship her as my master, or I won't get the intelligence I need to defeat her.*

His mind drifted back to the fight between Sakura and his grandfather in New York's Central Park. While humans wandered through the park on what they thought was a typical summer day, a major battle was going on just inches away—hidden from them by a magical shield.

What made him *so special?* Sakura had demanded of his grandfather. *Why did* he *get the power? The power that should have been mine? Who decided?*

That was obviously about me, but what did she mean by that? Mack wondered. *What power do I have that she doesn't?*

Mack was slowly beginning to realize that there was more going on in this war than a battle between teacher and student, good and evil. Sakura's rage went well beyond simply trying to surpass her old master. There was history. There was a deep hurt, a deep fury, that had been festering inside the Shadow Fox for a long time.

That must be what drove her to dark magic, he thought. *I'm going to have to find out what this is all about if the forces for good are going to prevail.*

Mack snapped back to reality and then blocked another attack from the *aatxe.* The battle was definitely going against them. He ordered a retreat.

Adam, a *nykur*—or Icelandic horse Changer who

could control lakes, rivers, and other waters—galloped over.

We're retreating again? he communicated. When in their animal forms, Changers spoke telepathically.

Even without spoken words, Mack heard the angry sneer in Adam's question. Mack said nothing but gave Adam a hard look.

Adam pushed the issue. *That's twice in one day. It's almost like you're not really on our side.*

Mack fought to keep fear from flitting across his features. If Sakura found out he was a double agent, she'd take him out, and any advantage the First Four had over her would be lost.

He turned on Adam with fiery eyes. *I'm giving it my—*

He was cut off when the *aatxe* charged at Adam and knocked him out.

Bingo, Mack thought privately.

With Adam unconscious and Sakura's forces already beginning to retreat from the battlefield, Mack finally felt it was safe to reach out to Ms. Therian.

I have intel for you, he told her. *Ask Gabriella to*

spirit-walk in my dreams tonight so I can pass the information along.

I'll do that, the werewolf told him.

They circled each other as if they were enemies about to enter hand-to-hand combat. Mack wished they were back at home in the Willow Cove gym, doing a training exercise.

Those days are over, Mack reminded himself. *You're at war.*

Adam began to stir.

The nykur suspects I'm working for the First Four. If Sakura finds out, I'm finished, Mack communicated. *She'll kill me, and you might lose this war.*

You need to prove your allegiance to the Shadow Fox, Ms. Therian answered. Attack me. It's the only way.

Attack you? No. I can't. I don't want to, Mack answered. He hadn't hurt anybody since becoming himself again. How could he?

Attack me, Mack, she repeated. *You have to. Any doubts Sakura has about you will be erased. We need her to trust you with her deepest secrets. It's the only way.*

Mack knew she was probably right, but he still hated

the thought of hurting her. He hated the thought of hurting anybody. But this was a dangerous game—and Mack had to play it right. He squared his shoulders and braced himself.

Sorry, Ms. Therian, Mack thought.

With Adam's eyes on him, Mack used a cloaking spell to make himself invisible. He circled his coach while she pretended to look for him. Then when the time was right, he pounced, unmasked himself, and sank his teeth into her leg.

He'd done it. He was behind enemy lines.

Chapter 3
INTEL

Gabriella grabbed two mugs from the cabinet and filled them with hot milk and chocolate. She'd just arrived home from New York City, and after the day's tumultuous events, it was finally time to relax.

"Can you make sure to add some marshmallows?" her little sister, Maritza, asked. "Tía Rosa never adds any marshmallows."

Gabriella smiled. There was so much her sister didn't know. She looked at Maritza and felt jealous for a moment, jealous that Maritza was concerned for her reading homework and her friends and sleepovers and elementary school. Maritza was wearing three friendship bracelets from her three best friends, and it all seemed like so much *fun*. Gabriella couldn't even imagine having time to make friendship bracelets with Darren, Fiona, and Mack. Never mind that Mack was currently double agenting in the belly of the beast, when would they possibly have time for something fun like that?

Gabriella found some mini-marshmallows in the pantry and some rainbow-colored sprinkles. "Let's make this unicorn hot chocolate," she told her sister, who loved all things fantastical—unicorns and mermaids and talking frogs.

If only she knew how magical the real world is, Gabriella thought.

"Unicorn hot chocolate!" Maritza gasped. She watched as Gabriella scooped a dollop of marshmallows into her mug.

"And the finishing touch," Gabriella said, opening the fridge door. "Whipped cream and sprinkles!"

Maritza clapped. "I have the best sister in the whole world," she said, taking a sip after Gabriella sprayed a mountain of whipped cream and topped it with sprinkles. A whipped cream mustache appeared on her upper lip, and Gabriella laughed, wiping it off with a kitchen towel.

Gabriella certainly didn't feel like the best sister in the world, though. When was the last time she and Maritza had hung out—like sisters? Perhaps before Gabriella had learned she was a *nahual*. So much had changed in seventh grade. Gabriella was hardly the person she was before.

"I have something important to tell you," Maritza said after a few sips. "I think I have a crush on someone in my class."

"A crush?" Gabriella's interest was piqued. "Who is it? Anyone I know?"

Maritza giggled. "A crush! A crush! But you have to *promise* to keep it a secret—Emma would *hate* me if she knew!"

Emma was one of Maritza's best friends.

"Okay, spill," Gabriella said. She was glad to have this family bonding. She missed it very much.

"Okay, so, we were sitting in the cafeteria at lunch, and Etai was walking past me, and I think he was the person who left me some secret Valentine's Day candy at my desk—oh, did I not tell you about that? Well, yeah, someone left secret Valentine's Day candy at my desk, and—and—"

But before Maritza could say anything else, her words were cut short. The kitchen door opened and in walked Tía Rosa, Gabriella and Maritza's aunt. Tía Rosa was also a *nahual*, along with Gabriela's *abuelita*, but Maritza (and their mother) didn't know.

A knot formed in Gabriella's stomach. Tía Rosa appearing unannounced and out of the blue—this had to be Changer news.

"Gabriella, a word?" Tía Rosa asked. "In private?"

Gabriella looked at Maritza. She so desperately wanted this sister time. But she had a duty; she knew what she had to do.

"One second," she told Maritza, and headed with Tía Rosa for the den.

Once there, Tía Rosa checked to make sure no one could hear her. She then drew the curtains closed just in case and spoke in muffled breaths.

"There's been another attack—this one close by," Tía Rosa informed her. "We have many Changers wounded.

I don't know much more than that. I need to be there to heal, so if you're looking for me—"

"What do you mean? I'm a healer too," Gabriella said. She didn't want to leave Maritza, but she had a duty, a sacred duty to the Changer nation. If Mack could be away from his family—and his friends—and work for the dark side . . . Gabriella had to help too.

"I'll get my stuff, Tía," Gabriella said. "Meet you outside in a minute."

Tía Rosa tried to protest, but it was no use. They both knew Gabriella had to help with the healing—whether she wanted to or not.

Gabriella went back into the kitchen and kissed the top of Maritza's head.

"Tía Rosa needs me," she said. "Ma is upstairs. If you put your mug in the sink when you're done, I'll wash it for you when I come back, okay, *mi linda*? I love you. I'll see you later."

Maritza looked sad. Gabriella wanted to stay, to hear about Etai and Emma and *normal* things, but she knew she couldn't. She laced up her combat boots and grabbed a protein bar. If she ever needed the extra energy from a protein bar, it was now. She cast a sidelong glance at her sister before leaving.

I feel so terrible for leaving her, Gabriella thought.

But that was the life of a Changer, wasn't it?

Gabriella and Tía Rosa arrived on the battleground in their *nahual* forms just as Sakura's forces retreated. It was clear that Gabriella made a good choice—healers were needed, and desperately.

Healing was something that only the most powerful of *nahuals* could do while spirit-walking in another Changer's mind. After their battle in New York City, Gabriella had started to learn how to heal others herself. Although difficult, it made all the difference when she used her new skills on Mack.

Gabriella had seen that Mack's dark magic wasn't something to be conquered like they'd thought—it was a deep pain that needed to be *healed*. She was able to use her power to overcome the darkness that Sakura had used to poison his mind and spirit. Mack was himself again—if only in secret—and determined to help win against Sakura.

It was the most amazing, terrifying, and gratifying thing she had ever done.

Gabriella looked around and saw just how much that healing was needed now. Everywhere she turned, it seemed a Changer was hurt.

Gabriella didn't know where to start. She looked among the wounded as if to assess who was in the most pain, to alleviate that pain first, when she caught sight of a woman's face in great agony.

But it wasn't just any woman. It was Ms. Therian.

Gabriella made a beeline toward her. She could see the deep pain in her coach's eyes and smell the burned skin around the wound on her leg. Gabriella barely had time to register that it was a *kitsune* bite mark before she got to work.

Gabriella gently placed her hands on either side of the wound and entered a meditative state. Almost immediately she could feel her spiritual energy begin to envelop the wound, and cast around for a path to recovery.

She reminded herself of what Daniel, the *nahual* who had taught her about healing, had said: *The body wants to heal itself. We're just helping it along.* She remembered to keep her energy loose and flexible—to follow where it led.

Gabriella expected Ms. Therian's wound to heal as easily as the injuries Daniel had mended. But this wound seemed to fighting her, as if it didn't want to give up its hold on Ms. Therian, almost like it was intended to be there, for some reason. Gabriella kept concentrating, letting her energy move about the injury, seeking a pathway to healing. She could tell her teacher was hurting, and Gabriella desperately wanted to lessen that pain.

It took a while, but the pain began to let go of its tight grip. Ms. Therian's skin finally began to knit itself back together. In a moment all traces of the bite and the burned skin around it were gone, but there was some lingering magic hovering around the area where the wound had been.

Gabriella had questions, but there were others who needed her help first. When she had done as much as she could for Ms. Therian, she came out of her meditative state and checked the battlefield. Tía Rosa was busy helping an *aatxe* with a broken leg while Margaery

Haruyama and Kenta, both *tengus*, transported three chained prisoners away in a ripple of wind.

Gabriella noticed a *bultungin* with a badly burned foot and leg. "I'll be right back," Gabriella told her teacher. "Rest here."

Ms. Therian nodded, and Gabriella headed off to help the other wounded Changers. As soon as she could, she made her way back to her coach's side. Tía Rosa was right behind her, offering support.

Ms. Therian moved her leg with a grimace. "Thank you, Gabriella," she said. "I feel so much better now."

"Was that a *kitsune* bite?" Gabriella asked. "Did Sakura—"

"No, I'm afraid this was not Sakura," Ms. Therian said quietly. "Mack."

"Mack?"

Gabriella was alarmed. What could have caused her friend to hurt their teacher? Had Sakura convinced him to go back to the dark side?

"I told him to do this. He really had no choice. One of Sakura's lieutenants was questioning Mack's loyalty," she explained. "Mack had to attack me if he was going to continue to be trusted by the Shadow Fox."

Gabriella sat back on her heels. "Poor Mack. He must have hated hurting you."

"It was necessary," Ms. Therian said, grimacing again. "And I'm a tough, old werewolf. But he did share something with me. He wants you to spirit-walk in his dreams tonight. He has some intelligence for us that he couldn't pass along on the battlefield."

"I'll be there," Gabriella said. "Is there a chance Sakura will find out what we're doing?"

"I don't think so, not while Mack is sleeping. And after today's attack on me, she'll trust him to resist you in any case," Ms. Therian said.

I hope she's right, Gabriella thought.

Sometimes it felt like the fate of this whole war rested on Gabriella's ability to spirit-walk in Mack's mind, or his ability to fool Sakura into believing he was still her apprentice in mind, body, and soul. Where was Fiona? Or Darren?

Gabriella didn't mean to be resentful, but it was a big responsibility. She regretted leaving Maritza behind so much. All she could think of was *her* unicorn hot chocolate, growing cold on the kitchen counter. And had it been only a year ago that Gabriella was concerned about making the soccer team?

Tía Rosa placed her palm over Ms. Therian's leg, feeling the magical energy emanate from it. "That was a really powerful bite—probably a lot more powerful than Mack realized. You're going to need a few days of rest to heal fully."

"Only if Sakura's army will give us that time," Ms. Therian answered. "We have to defeat her at every juncture. We can't rest. Not now, not ever."

Tía Rosa opened her mouth to object but then saw the determined look on Ms. Therian's face. "Let's hope they need to do some healing too," she said. "I think we got the better of them—again. You need to stay off this leg as much as you can."

Ms. Therian nodded but didn't comment. Her mind was already on the next task. "Let's hurry back to our Changer base in Willow Cove and see what's going on," she said. "I am worried about them. Sakura might have attacked there too."

A second later Margaery returned. She stood in the center of the group and made sure that each Changer had a hand on her. There was a *whoosh*, and for a moment Gabriella felt like she was nestled inside a gust of wind. For two or three dizzying seconds the world flew by, and then they landed gently in the Changer base underneath the Willow Cove house Mack shared with his grandfather. The base was a safe place for Changers to gather when there was trouble. Enchantments kept it from human eyes and from evil forces.

Gabriella sighed. She wished they were returning home, so she could be with Maritza, but she understood why she couldn't.

When they arrived Gabriella was surprised to find people waiting for them—Mr. Kimura; Fiona; Darren; and Darren's brother, Ray.

Then she did a double take.

Ray?

What was he doing there?

He wasn't a Changer!

Ray looked just as shocked as Gabriella. "*Her* too?" he asked, pointing at Gabriella. Then he half smiled at

Darren. "No wonder why my little bro has been so popular with the ladies lately."

Really? Gabriella thought. She knew Darren sometimes felt alone, but things were bad enough without bringing a nonmagical human—*especially* one who makes really bad jokes—into the circle.

"What's *he* doing here?" Gabriella snapped. She immediately regretted her harsh tone, but things were already stressful enough without a non-Changer to protect.

"Hey, I'm one of you now, I guess," Ray said with a smile. Gabriella shot him a glare. "A . . . a Change-ler thing," Ray said.

"Changer," Gabriella said, but her tone was a bit less harsh this time.

"When I got home from New York, Ray was just discovering his powers," Darren explained. "He was going kind of wild—like I did when electricity first started crackling at my fingertips."

Gabriella eyed Ray. There didn't seem to be any electricity around him now.

"I've borrowed Ray's *impundulu* abilities, while he

learns about control," Mr. Kimura explained.

"Changers can do that?" Gabriella asked. She felt like she was learning new things about Changer powers all the time.

"It's an advanced *kitsune* skill that only powerful *kitsune* can perform," Ms. Therian told her. "However, borrowed abilities can be difficult to control, even for someone as advanced as Akira."

It was only then that Gabriella noticed that Mr. Kimura was concentrating very intensely, as if he was fighting not to let the lightning loose. Then she spotted Fiona. The hair on the left side of her head was about eight inches shorter than the hair on the right side, though she didn't seem to mind.

"What happened to your hair?" Gabriella asked.

Fiona smiled. "A little haircut courtesy of the *impundulu* salon," she joked. "Looks like I'll have to wear a wig for a while, just so no one will freak."

Gabriella laughed. She actually kind of liked Fiona's new 'do.

Gabriella was happy to have some relatively chill time with Fiona and Darren, but it hit her that she hadn't seen other friends in weeks. Never mind soccer practice. Never mind family time.

Gabriella was proud to be a Changer. But at what cost?

———

Once everything was clear, Gabriella and Tía Rose headed home. Maritza was already asleep. Gabriella did the dishes; poured out her stale, now-watery hot chocolate; then crawled into bed. She was exhausted, but somehow still, had more to do—she couldn't sleep until she had connected with Mack. She needed to spirit-walk in his dreams.

Gabriella entered a meditative state and immediately began casting a wide net with her spiritual energy, searching for Mack. Thankfully, her Mack intuition was good—she found him a few minutes later. He was dreaming about a comic-book convention.

There was a huge poster announcing the newest installment of The Emerald Wildcat, a comic book they had worked on together. Fans were dressed in costume and clamoring for autographed copies while holding the latest issue. In the dream, Gabriella sat next to him at a table, signing comic books for happy readers. A giant blowup of a magazine article called the two of them "Mack and Gabriella—Comics' New Dream Team."

Mack turned and saw Gabriella. He greeted her with a big smile. His dream faded into the background but didn't disappear entirely.

I *wonder if that's part of his masking illusion,* Gabriella wondered. Then she realized it must be. Mack was very smart. It was a good idea too.

"You're here," Mack said. "I'm having good dreams again, thanks to you. Before you healed me, all I had were nightmares."

"I'm glad," Gabriella said. "Well, not about the nightmares. About you having good dreams again."

"How is Ms. Therian?" Mack asked.

"I healed her wound," Gabriella told him. "She'll be good as new in a few days."

"Biting her was horrible," Mack said. "Please tell her how sorry I am."

"It was necessary, she said," Gabriella answered. "She knows you're sorry, anyway. How is everything else going? Ms. Therian said someone suspected you of being a double agent."

Mack shrugged. "A *nykur* named Adam. He's jealous of my connection with Sakura, but the important thing is that *she* doesn't suspect me. And she doesn't. Especially after I attacked Ms. Therian. You should have seen how happy she was when I told her."

"That's good," Gabriella said. "She can't find out you're one of us again."

"There's still something I don't know about Sakura, though," Mack admitted. "Something important. It might be the key to everything that's happening. There's a secret hidden here, somewhere. Something that has to do with me."

"Is that your intel?" Gabriella asked. "Do you want me to ask your grandfather what it could be? Sorry to cut to the chase. I'm worried if I stay too long, we'll be discovered," she added.

"No, that's not it. I wish it were. In the coming few days, Sakura is planning a sneak attack on the *selkies*," Mack said. "But I don't have any specific details. There are a couple of traitors in the *selkie* faction—I couldn't find out what their names are, but at least one is in Queen Leana's inner circle. Warn Fiona. She and her mother need to try to figure out who the traitors are and what they're planning. I'm not sure how much time they have. The attack could be just days away."

"I'll warn them," Gabriella said earnestly. An attack on the *selkies*? That was definitely bad news. "Thanks, Mack. Be safe."

"You too," Mack told her. There was a beat of silence. Gabriella knew there was more Mack wanted to say— he must have felt so alone—but it wasn't safe to get personal.

With that, Gabriella spirit-walked out of Mack's dream. She tried to will herself to get out of bed and find her *tía* Rosa, to share the news immediately, but after the events of the day, her arms and legs felt like lead weights. She fought to open her eyes, but lost that battle.

It'll be okay, she told herself. *Mack said the attack would be days away. I can warn Fiona in the morning. I can help everyone in the morning. I can . . . I need . . . some . . . rest. . . .*

Chapter 4
Underwater

After the night's events, Mr. Kimura brought Fiona back home. She entered the house to find both her mother and her father sitting at the kitchen table, arms folded. They didn't exactly look . . . happy.

"Fiona," her father said sharply. He was never this stern, and Fiona could tell she was in big trouble. "Your mother tells me that you ran out on an important discussion with her earlier today—and directly into a lightning storm."

"We've been worried," her mother added. "It's been hours with no word from you."

"I had to make sure Darren was safe," Fiona said.

She wasn't quite sure how to tell her father about ancient curses. "He was fine, but . . . well, there were developments."

"Developments or not, we have to make sure *you* are safe," her mother said. Then she reached up and touched Fiona's much shorter hair. She could sense something was off. "Your hair's been touched with Changer magic. What happened?"

Fiona didn't dare say that a wayward bolt of lightning had chopped it off. She shrugged. "I wanted a change. Gabriella did it for me." That wasn't exactly a lie. Gabriella and her *tía* Rosa had helped Fiona even it out while the First Four discussed things. They had even added layers. Fiona thought she looked great.

But her new look wasn't enough to change the subject for long.

"You can't run off like that whenever you feel like it," her father said.

"But—"

"But nothing," Fiona's mother said, cutting her off. "With Sakura's forces planning who knows what, we need to know where you are and that you're safe at all times."

"My friends needed me," Fiona answered. "The First Four needed me."

"They need you to *be safe*, Fee. They need you to be accepted by the *selkies*, so you can bring the two groups together again. Neither of those things will happen if the *selkies* think of you as a traitor."

Leana leaned forward and took Fiona's hand. "I know you want to stay with your friends, but this is what has to happen—for your safety and for your friends'. You have to visit the *selkies* like we talked about—*before* you ran off."

Fiona slumped in a chair, frustrated. She was being pulled in too many directions. Her duty to her mother pulled her in one direction, and her duty to the First Four pulled her in another. And of course there was her nonmagical father, who worried more with each revelation about unrest in the Changer world.

At least Sakura's forces are on the run, Fiona thought. *Maybe we'll have some time to regroup before the next battle. If I have to leave my friends for a bit, it might as well be when Sakura is resting.*

Reluctantly, Fiona agreed. "I'll go with you. But if the

First Four need me, I have to come back. You must know that you can't stop me. Period."

Fiona's mother couldn't hide her smile.

"We'll leave first thing in the morning," she said, kissing Fiona on the forehead. "I'm sorry to pull you away. But trust me. It's for the best."

Fiona noticed that her mother didn't address the second part of her statement, that she'd come back if the First Four needed her, but she was too tired to argue anymore. She said good night and headed upstairs to her room and her bed.

Maybe it is okay for me to go away for a few days, she thought. *After all, Sakura's army was forced to retreat twice today. And if Mack's intel is urgent, I'll hear from Gabriella before I leave.*

Early the next morning Fiona checked herself out in the mirror over her dresser. *I'm rocking this new hairstyle,* she thought. She'd had long flowing hair for as long as she could remember. Making this change made her feel, well, *cool,* and maybe even a little more powerful. And even with everything else going on, she felt lighter without all that hair weighing her down.

She smiled. She was about to text Gabriella and Darren to let them know she'd be with the *selkie*s for a few days. Then she remembered it was supposed to be a secret—even from the First Four. Fiona wasn't used to keeping secrets from them.

Her mother knocked and came into her room. "I wanted to wish you luck today," Leana said.

Fiona pointed to her bookshelves, crammed with books. "I don't believe in luck," she said. "I believe in reading and in numbers and in careful analysis, not to mention strength. Luck isn't real."

Leana laughed. "Haven't you ever heard the phrase the 'luck of the Irish'?" she asked.

Fiona nodded. "Of course, but that doesn't mean—"

"Luck is real, my darling girl," Leana said with a smile. "Luck is very, very real."

She started to sing a new song, one Fiona hadn't heard before. And she couldn't help but notice that the song didn't flow as smoothly from her mother's lips as most of the other songs filled with *selkie* magic.

There's something different about this song, Fiona

thought. *It doesn't have the same rhythms of the waves and the tides as most magical songs.*

Leana sang the song all the way through and then repeated it, having Fiona join her in the second round. As Fiona sang, she felt the song move through her, but like her mother's, her words were halting. They didn't flow as freely as the other *selkie* songs—songs that had become a part of her.

"This is the most powerful, rarest song I know," Fiona's mother told her when she finished.

"More powerful than the Queen's Song?" Fiona asked. It didn't seem possible.

Leana nodded. "The Queen's Song calls upon the past *selkie* queens for help and protection. This is the Amhrán Sinsear—the song that calls upon your *non-magical* ancestors to ask for their help."

"But if they don't have magic, how much help can they be?" Fiona asked.

"Everyone has magic," her mother answered. "But not everyone can *use* their magic. Only very special *selkies* can tap into the strength of their nonmagical ancestors and use it for good. I believe you're one of them.

"Many *selkies* *know* this song, but few of us can *perform* it—including me," Leana continued. "But I believe you can master this. And if you can make the words in the Amhrán Sinsear flow freely from your lips, my darling Fiona, you can bring good luck and excellent fortune to anyone you choose."

Fiona couldn't hide her surprise. *Selkies* almost always married other *selkies*. Since her father wasn't magical, Fiona was unusual and unique in the *selkie* world. Even though she was heir to the *selkie* throne, other waterborne Changers were sometimes surprised by her strength and power. It was as if they expected her to have just half of the abilities of an average magical being.

I *might actually have an ability that even my powerful mother doesn't have*, she thought proudly. *One that draws on the support of my father's—nonmagical—ancestors.*

Suddenly, the idea of using or having luck wasn't so unrealistic after all.

Fiona was so busy turning over this new idea that she headed downstairs to the kitchen without checking her phone. Not that it mattered, anyway. Leana wanted

Fiona's phone to stay upstairs—it wouldn't work from deep within the sea.

Little did she know, while Fiona was eating her eggs Florentine and buttered toast, Gabriella was sending an urgent text from across town:

> Sakura poised to attack the selkie isles. Warn your mother. Traitor in her midst.

After saying good-bye to her father and promising not to do anything reckless (*More reckless than visiting the selkies?* Fiona thought), Fiona and her mother walked across the street to the cliff's edge and made their way down the steep stairs leading to the water.

Fiona had one last wish that she could let her friends know where she was going, but her mother had said it wasn't safe. On that she wouldn't be budged.

With the rising sun shining on the waves, they donned their *selkie* cloaks and transformed for the swim to the Isles of Saorsie, the *selkie* lands.

Fiona loved being in the ocean. She felt completely free and at home. She loved the rhythm and the pulse of the waves, the pull of the tides, and the way the sun danced on the surface of the sea. She dove in and out of the waves, forgetting the Shadow Fox, forgetting the First Four, even forgetting her friends. Swimming made her feel free and full of joy.

Their journey took about a half a day. She and her mother stopped to rest on a sandbar just off the coast of the Isle of Saorsie and transformed back into their human selves. A group of young *selkies* about Fiona's age were sunning themselves nearby. Fiona noticed they were watching the two of them while pretending to look elsewhere. Her first thought was that there might be a problem.

I'm being silly. My mother is the queen, Fiona told herself. *Of course they're interested in her.*

Leana noticed too. "The *selkies* your age are curious about you," she said. "Why don't you stay and make some new friends?"

Curious—about *Fiona*?

Fiona was embarrassed to admit that the very idea of approaching girls her own age made her nervous. Making friends had never been easy for her. She was the loner, smart girl in all the advanced classes at school, the one who got along better with her teachers than her classmates. The other kids were nice—she was never bullied or anything like that—but they never really *clicked*. She would sit alone on the bus, and in the cafeteria at lunchtime, reading. She told herself that it didn't matter, that it simply meant she had extra time for her studies. But once in a while she'd hear other girls talk about a birthday party they had been to, or a movie, or going out to eat, and a wave of sadness would wash over her for a moment before she'd return to her books.

Learning that she was a Changer had made everything different. Fiona, Darren, Gabriella, and Mack had become fast friends through their shared bond, and she enjoyed having kids her own age to hang out with and talk to for the first time. But the idea of getting to know new girls—new *selkie* girls—was still a little scary, if not downright terrifying.

What if they don't like me? What if I'm the loner girl all over again?

"I'll leave you alone," Leana said. "Go and introduce yourself."

Her mother sensed Fiona's hesitation.

"You're their princess," she reminded her. "They

want to know you. Stop by the castle when you are done."

Fiona took a deep breath and nodded.

The girls bowed as Leana passed them by, then turned to Fiona.

"Hi," Fiona said nervously. "I'm Fiona."

The girls introduced themselves. The tallest one was Aiyana. There was also Sibeal and Moira.

They seem nervous too, Fiona thought. *Maybe I'm not the only one who is nervous about meeting new people.*

"Your hair is so cool," Sibeal blurted out.

Fiona noticed that they all had long flowing locks just like hers had been.

"I just got it cut," she said with a laugh, running her hand through it. "I'm still getting used to it."

"I love it," Aiyana said with a smile. "I want to cut my hair too, but I can't because of the school play."

"The school play!" Moira said, clearly very alarmed. "We're late for rehearsal!"

"I'm not in any of today's scenes; you two go. Break a leg!" Aiyana said. The other two girls left, apologizing profusely, while Aiyana stayed behind. Luckily, Aiyana wanted to be Fiona's friend as much as Fiona wanted to be hers. She was filled with questions about Fiona's life among the humans. "I've spent my whole life with the *selkies*," Aiyana said. "I don't think I've ever even talked to a human."

I've made a new friend! Fiona thought. *It's not like she has to be nice to me because we're thrown together all the time the way Gabriella, Darren, and Mack are. Aiyana really wants to be my friend!*

As Fiona expected from a youngling *selkie*, it wasn't long before Aiyana brought the conversation around to the First Four. She didn't ask Fiona if the rumors about her being one of the next First Four were true, but she volunteered an important fact about herself.

"It's not popular, but I support the First Four," she whispered to Fiona. "I hope we can all come together again, peacefully."

"I hope so too," Fiona said. "But you're the first *selkie* I've met who feels that way."

Aiyana smiled at her, her eyes wide and unguarded. "The *selkies* have been separate from the rest of the Changer world for far too long. I'd like to see us mingle.

If nothing else, we'll get to learn about new hairstyles," she said with a laugh.

She means what she says, Fiona thought. *Perhaps things aren't as bad as they seem. Maybe the selkies will come around to our way of thinking more easily than my mother believes.*

Fiona and Aiyana continued to talk about their favorite places to swim and Aiyana's *selkie* school and how good new books smell. Fiona felt good. Maybe her mother was right after all!

Chapter 5
THE NEW IMPUNDULU

It had been a while since Darren had gotten to ride his bike. He hadn't even noticed. His Changer duties took up so much of his day, he'd completely forgotten. Alas, when Darren hopped on his bike to head to Greasy Dan's Palace, Ray's favorite fast-food joint, his legs were stiff at first. Then it all fell into place again. Darren wished his life could be like that—a second of confusion, then ease.

But of course, Darren was a Changer, and life didn't exactly work like that.

Darren had left Ray at the Changer base overnight for safekeeping and told his mother that Ray was sleeping in his apartment near the New Brighton college campus. He hated lying to his mom, but it was easy enough—and after all, Ray *was* an adult.

Darren grabbed Ray's favorite greasy egg sandwich for breakfast and exactly five ketchup packets (Ray was particular, to say the least) and slung them into his messenger bag. Then he pedaled to the Changer base to meet Ray. But he was surprised to find his brother sitting at the Kimura kitchen table talking to someone else—and not just any someone else. Professor Zwane.

Darren had first met Professor Zwane, a professor of African tribal mythology, in the spring at Wyndemere Academy, the only boarding school in the country for Changers. Darren had visited the campus with his friends to participate in the Youngling Games—and also to see if he wanted to go there for high school. It was then that Darren learned of the *anansi* curse on his bloodline.

"Darren. You did it. The curse is lifted," Professor Zwane said when Darren took off his helmet and headed in.

Before Darren could ask how he knew, the professor responded.

"Akira Kimura contacted me. I have to admit, with

everything going on, it's nice to have some good news. Now I can perform the protection spell that failed because of the curse. You *and* your brother will both be protected from Sakura's mind control."

Ray looked confused. Darren, with Ms. Therian and Mr. Kimura's help, had given Ray as much information as he could handle last night, but adding in the fact that there was a mysterious *kitsune* villain out there who was capable of mind control seemed maybe like too much to handle.

Darren thought about how that would sound. *Hey, bro, welcome to your new powers and new life. Now get ready to go to war. Oh, and by the way, you could lose power over your mind, too.*

Now he saw the question in Ray's eyes and shook his head. "I'll explain later," Darren told him. "It's kind of a long story."

Professor Zwane's spell was an ancient one that predated written language and drew on the power of Darren and Ray's *impundulu* ancestors to guard and protect them.

They walked into the living room just after Ray gobbled down his sandwich. Ray made a face while

Professor Zwane set out the materials he needed—all provided by the First Four recently, when Zwane originally tried to cast the spell. Mr. Kimura had contributed an ivory bowl covered in ancient runes. Into it the professor poured a leftover jar of blue whale's milk from Yara, red sand from the deserts of Babylon from Sefu, and a rare savanna herb contributed by Ms. Therian. He would use them to call on Darren and Ray's ancestors and ask them to protect the brothers.

Darren took a deep breath. The smell tickled his nose. He had to stifle a laugh, picturing himself sneezing all over his ghostly ancestors.

The professor laid three pillows in a circle on the floor. He sat cross-legged on one and motioned for Darren and Ray to take the others. Then he placed the ivory bowl in the middle of them, closed his eyes, and began to chant in an ancient language Darren had heard only once before: the time the spell had failed.

Will it work today? Darren wondered, realizing, not for the first time, he was nervous. Doubly nervous, if he was being honest. *Now I have to worry about Ray as well as myself.*

A warm glow began to emanate from the bowl. It

grew to surround Darren, Ray, and the professor. Darren sat bathed in the light for a moment, feeling calm and supported. In an instant all his nervousness disappeared and he felt good.

It's so peaceful. Is Ray feeling this too? he wondered. He opened his eyes to check and saw shadows all around them. Men and women were smiling and reaching for him and for Ray. Nothing about them was frightening. It was all so welcome.

The shadows of my ancestors, Darren thought, *here to protect Ray and me.*

Their touch was comforting, but this time Darren sensed something else. Something warm yet gentle. *Gratitude,* he realized after a moment. *They're grateful that the curse is lifted.*

Ray was looking around and smiling, and Darren felt his own face break into a grin as well. His ancestors' joy was contagious. He could tell they had wanted to come through the first time, too.

Darren wondered if he should speak to thank them but was afraid to break the spell. He closed his eyes and thought the words.

A moment later the shadows dissipated along with the glow from the bowl.

"Wow," Ray said. "That was amazing. Were they all *impundulus*?"

Professor Zwane nodded. "Not all were able to transform in their lifetimes because of the curse, but they were all meant to be *impundulus*. They must feel free at last."

Mr. Kimura stepped forward then. Darren hadn't even known he had joined them.

"I believe Ray will be better able to handle his powers now, with your help," Mr. Kimura said to Darren and Professor Zwane. "Time and patience. Patience and time. And some ancestors offering their blessings. I'm ready to give his powers back to him."

Darren noticed the fatigue etched into the man's face. Borrowing Ray's powers had taken a lot out of him, especially on top of his worries about Mack and the entire Changer world. Now Mr. Kimura placed his hands on Ray's shoulders and chanted a few magical words.

Darren watched an electrical charge pass through Mr. Kimura to Ray. A second later Ray sat up straighter.

Sparks traveled up and down his body, but this time they settled into his skin.

"I did it!" Ray said. "I controlled the lightning."

"You did," Darren said with a smile. "That was great."

Mr. Kimura left them to it, and the brothers trained together under the professor's direction. Darren demonstrated move after move.

Although Ray was new to his *impundulu* power, he was much more advanced than Darren had been when he just started.

"Ray has been training to change his whole life," Professor Zwane said. "He just didn't know it. He's had years and years of this. Mental preparation. Perhaps he's even ready to try transforming for the first time."

Darren gulped. It had taken him a while to transform. But he also understood what Professor Zwane was saying.

Darren stood up and first showed Ray how he transformed and then changed back. How he blended Darren the human with Darren the bird. Ray saw his brother Change, and his eyes went wide.

"Whoa," he said. "I guess I can start calling you birdbrain from now on?"

"Only if you're Birdbrain Number Two," said Darren.

"Hey! I'm Birdbrain Number One!" Ray shouted.

Ray mimicked Darren's movements exactly. Darren noticed that Professor Zwane was right—Ray *was* ready to transform, despite being, technically, a youngling.

In one elegant sweep Ray transformed. He was a fierce *impundulu*, with a massive wingspan. After a few moments Professor Zwane spoke.

"We don't want to overdo it on your very first day," he said. "Change back."

Ray did as he was told.

"You know, I always felt there was something missing from my life," Ray said. "Something missing from me. I thought it might have something to do with being black in a mostly white town, or with the fact that Mom and Dad didn't have the happiest marriage in the world. But now I know it was these . . . these *magical powers* I wasn't able to access. They should be scary and terrifying, but somehow, I feel like I'm more myself than I ever have been." His words were beautiful but Darren couldn't relate.

"I didn't feel that way when I first found out," Darren

admitted. "I just felt scared. And like a total mutant. The first time I transformed, I did it in my sleep. I flew right out of my bedroom window and came to in my human form in the middle of a field. Luckily, Mr. Kimura figured out what was happening, found me, and brought me home. But I was really freaked out. I just wanted the whole thing to go away, so I could be a normal kid again."

"Now I understand that bizarre lightning storm that sat over our house the night Mom and Dad told us they were getting a divorce," Ray said.

Darren grimaced. "I wanted to be able to talk to you about what I was going through more than anything, but . . ."

"You couldn't. I get that. I would have thought you were out of your mind," Ray said. "And you got through it on your own."

"Not all alone for the most part. I had lots of help from my friends and the First Four, and later, the professor," Darren said. "Now I couldn't imagine being without my powers or the other Changers, but it was definitely weird at first."

Professor Zwane nodded. "You're one of the most

talented young *impundulus* I've met, Darren. I hope you're proud of yourself."

"You should be, bro," Ray said. Then he grinned. "You broke a thousand-year-old curse and turned me into a *bird*."

Darren started to laugh. "And I'm *still* only Birdbrain Number Two," he joked.

The brothers laughed. Then Professor Zwane took on a more serious note.

"Ray, I've been watching you today. I can sense that you have a different power from Darren," he said. "It's a bit puzzling, actually. I can feel the same powerful *impundulu* bloodline coursing through you, but there's something else."

"Something else?" Ray asked.

Professor Zwane nodded.

"It's rare but not entirely unheard of. I think you have the power to curse a Changer—and all of that Changer's descendants—much like the *anansi* did to your family. As a result of your powers lying dormant for so long. The powers know, almost . . . like the curse is bound into them, still."

Whoa, Darren thought. *Ray has the power to curse other Changers? That's extreme.*

Ray looked horrified for a moment. "I'd never do that," Ray said. "I'd never curse another Changer. I'd hate to think of someone else living their life feeling the way I did—that something was missing or that they weren't enough. It's terrible."

Darren wasn't so sure. *What if someone is really bad—evil, even? Shouldn't they have their powers cursed to keep them from doing damage that can't be reversed?*

He wanted to think about that a bit more before he debated his big brother, though. He knew *all* about getting into brotherly arguments without the proper preparation—it usually meant he got the shorter end of the stick.

Darren was relieved when Mr. Kimura ambled over with a wooden tea tray.

Mr. Kimura set the teakettle, cups, and plate of little pancake sandwiches with cream in the center of the group.

"These are *dorayaki,*" Mr. Kimura said. "Ancient Japanese dessert."

Ray and Darren had each eaten two before Mr. Kimura even poured the tea.

"These are delicious—even better than the egg sandwich Darren brought me," Ray said. "I didn't know you were a chef."

"I'm not," Mr. Kimura said with a smile. His eyes filled with longing. "This recipe belonged to Makoto's mother, my daughter-in-law. She was an excellent baker."

"She certainly was," Ray said through a mouthful of *dorayaki*. "Did she leave you any other recipes you want to try out on us? Maybe something with bananas? I love bananas."

"She wanted to be sure I had this particular recipe before she died. I'm afraid I have no others," Mr. Kimura responded.

Darren looked up, suddenly interested.

She wanted him to have this recipe before she died?

Mack said that his parents died in a car accident when he was small. But Mr. Kimura's words made it seem like his mother was preparing, almost . . . giving away her favorite recipes. That certainly wasn't something a healthy new mother would do, was it?

"I thought Mack's parents died in a car crash," Darren said.

For a second he *almost* saw Mr. Kimura's face pale a bit. But before he could answer, Darren's phone started to vibrate with an incoming text.

"It's from Gabriella," Darren said, clicking on the message.

> Urgent. Got some intel from Mack. Where's Fiona? She's not answering her phone.

Chapter 6
THE AMHRÁN SINSEAR

Fiona spent the whole afternoon with Aiyana, talking about everything and anything. Aiyana was a bookworm like her. They liked all of the same stories. And she loved history. Most importantly, they both loved pineapple pizza.

Fiona was careful, however, not to mention her connection with the First Four. Although her mother made it seem like most *selkies* knew, she'd been instructed not to talk about it.

I hope Aiyana isn't insulted when she does find out, Fiona thought.

After half a day with Aiyana, having fun and just

hanging out, Fiona joined her mother at the *selkie* palace for dinner.

She was positively bubbling with news and information.

"Mom! I made a new friend—Aiyana," Fiona said excitedly.

"Aiyana?" her mother said. "I can't remember a youngling *selkie* with that name." She looked concerned for a moment but then shook it off. "But that's nothing to worry about— I don't know the names of every single *selkie*, as much as I'd like to. If you like her, then I like her." She smiled.

After dinner they practiced the Amhrán Sinsear a bit more. It was a song Leana herself struggled with. Fiona thought she had it at first, but the more she practiced the song, the harder it seemed to get. Eventually, she threw up her arms in frustration.

"Nothing I've ever learned has been this hard," Fiona said. "And that includes calculus!"

Leana chuckled.

But Fiona wasn't laughing. She kept trying and failing. It was only then that she realized some of her mother's council members were in the palace—listening. She could almost hear their thoughts. She imagined what they were thinking—that she was too inexperienced, too inadequate.

Fiona felt her face getting red. *I have to get this right,* she thought. *Not just to prove that I can, but to bring good luck to all my friends and help the Changers win the war against Sakura. But what if I can't learn the song in time? What will happen then?*

Her mother noticed that Fiona was getting flustered and looked at her kindly.

"Take a break," Leana told Fiona gently. "It'll come in time, but you can't force it. Go and have some fun."

Fiona swam to the water's edge. Her mother was right—she needed to find some time for herself. Fiona was surprised to find Aiyana still at the water's edge. Aiyana had a slice of pizza with her, and they shared it and laughed.

"I needed that," Fiona said. "I've been trying to learn a new song, and I was getting so frustrated."

"Which one?" Aiyana asked.

"The Amhrán Sinsear," Fiona said. "It's important. And it's *hard.*"

"It is," Aiyana said. "It took me a while to master it."

"You've mastered it?" Fiona asked incredulously. She tried to hide her surprise, but she saw something flit across Aiyana's face.

Did I insult her? Mom told me it was a rare skill, but maybe Aiyana is special. I hope I didn't make her feel bad.

Fiona changed the subject. "I love being a *selkie*," she said, leaning back with a sigh. "I was always drawn to the sea, always loved it. When I found out I was a *selkie* it all made perfect sense somehow."

Aiyana nodded. "I've always known I was a *selkie*, of course, because I was born and raised here. But when I came into my abilities I discovered I was a skinwalker, too. And that made a kind of weird sense. I always felt like I could try on other people's lives—walk around in them and get to know them from the inside out."

"What's a skinwalker?" Fiona asked.

"Skinwalkers can transform into any animal, not just their Changer forms. All I need is that animal's pelt or cloak, and I can become that. It's pretty amazing," Aiyana said.

If only I had a skill like that, I'd be a better leader, Fiona thought. *Maybe when I'm one of the new First Four, Aiyana will help us learn more about the various factions. She can help us make peace with them.*

"It sounds amazing," Fiona said.

"It is, and because I can be any Changer form, I learned how to upgrade the Amhrán Sinsear by adding a verse in Gaelic."

Gaelic? Fiona couldn't speak Gaelic. She hesitated, but as she did, Aiyana started to sing the verse, and the words sounded beautiful.

Where could the harm be in such beauty? Fiona thought. *Mom probably just wanted me to master the rest of the song before telling me about this upgraded verse. Mack always complains that his grandfather is like that. But if it helps defeat Sakura, I think it's worth it.*

Slowly, with repetition, Fiona memorized the new verse. She liked the melody it came with. It sounded like the tide of the ocean, mixed with the power of something else.

Fiona was surprised. The Gaelic words came easier than the ones she could understand.

Maybe that's the trick, Fiona thought with a grin. *If*

you have no idea what the words mean, the song rolls off your tongue more smoothly!

Fiona practiced it again and again. She was thankful to Aiyana for helping her. And she was thankful if this would help them win the Changer War.

Chapter 7
KITSUNE BLOODLINES

Mack was at Sakura's main base. Until today, she had been very hard on him, demanding that he constantly prove his loyalty to her. But today, after his attack on Ms. Therian, she seemed to have accepted him and was much nicer. Instead of listening to one of Adam's relentless attacks on Mack, she bound the *nykur's* mouth closed with a flick of her finger.

Ms. Therian *was right*, he thought. *Sakura doesn't doubt my allegiance now.*

"My young apprentice, by taking down Dorina Therian, you have proven yourself," she hissed. "You have pledged yourself to me—most importantly, you have pledged yourself to *your* power."

Mack bowed with a smile. "It was my pleasure, Master."

"Remember—our quest for domination is not yet complete," she hissed. "Not until the old man goes down, too."

Mack was careful to keep his expression blank. The "old man" was his grandfather, the person he loved more than anyone else in the world.

A sly smile crossed Sakura's face. "We *will* succeed. We *must* succeed. Do you understand?"

Mack nodded. "Of course, Master. It's the only thing I desire—to succeed for *you*."

He wanted to cringe when he said it.

"You and I will rule the Changer world. All others will worship at our feet."

To prove her point, she gave Adam a kick, forcing him to his knees.

Even though Mack hated Adam, it was hard to watch. Mack reminded himself to tap into the Shadow Fox's wickedness.

"The old man held me back," Mack sneered. "Constantly telling me to wait. Telling me I wasn't ready to fully tap into my abilities, to learn powerful magic. Not like you, Master. You always know what's best for me. For me and for my power. I've learned more from you in these few weeks than I would learn in years from the old man."

Sakura smiled for real this time. "You are very wise, my young apprentice," she said. "And I will reward that wisdom in our new Changer dominion. As a token of my generosity, whatever you want, you shall have. You have one free gift."

"Thank you, Master," Mack said. "I will think very carefully about this generous gift."

Was Sakura really offering Mack a gift? Any one thing he wanted? What Mack really wanted was to give up the war, to be reunited with his friends and with his grandfather. But he couldn't tell Sakura that, of course.

Mack thought a bit. There *was* something he wanted, something he had started to think about far before the war began. And it was the perfect thing to ask from her—to take her away.

"I'd like to visit Japan," Mack blurted out loud. "I'd

like to see where my parents were born and where the *kitsune* are from."

Sakura bristled. "Your parents mean nothing—weakling *kitsune* they were," she said, "but I see your curiosity, my young apprentice. You shall see the birthplace of the most powerful of Changer-kind. There's no need to wait for our victory. We'll go now—together."

She snapped her fingers, and a *tengu* arrived. *Is it really that simple?* Mack thought. For Sakura, it was.

Moments later Sakura and Mack were looking up at an old house on the top of a hill—in Japan.

Mack stood frozen for a moment. The house had been savagely ripped apart, but what remained took his breath away. Walls, each one painted with a bold and beautiful portrait of a *kitsune*, were the only elements of the house still standing.

This is like the coolest comic book art I've ever seen, Mack thought. He slowly walked up the hill, forgetting all about Sakura and Willow Cove for a moment. *Except these aren't comics.* The *kitsune* looked real—like they could leap off the walls.

Mack wandered from portrait to portrait, only

slowly remembering that Sakura was right behind him.

"Who drew these?" Mack asked. "Do you know?"

Sakura squared her shoulders and stood a little taller.

"I did," she said. "Have I never told you that I'm an artist?"

I *had no idea*, Mack thought. *Art is something* I *love too.* He had no idea that he and the Shadow Fox had something in common.

Mack pointed to a portrait of a red fox with four tails that was about to leap off the wall. "Can you tell me what's happening in these paintings?" he asked.

"This is the house where the old man trained me," Sakura said. "Where he kept me as a *prisoner*. Magic kept me locked inside while your grandfather pushed and pushed. My one solace was creating these paintings. Now I return to them every now and then, as a reminder."

Mack remained silent. *That's not the grandfather I know,* he thought. *Either Jiichan has changed or Sakura's memories have been twisted and poisoned by her evil magic, just like she poisoned mine.*

"These paintings represent the original *kitsune*

bloodlines," Sakura continued. "*Kitsune* were among the first of Circe's Changers, the first people granted transformative magic."

Mack's grandfather and the others had taught him all about Changer history, but very little about *kitsune* history. Gabriella had learned about *nahual* history from her aunt and her grandmother, and Fiona was getting instruction in *selkie* history from her mother. Even Darren—who had no *impundulu* relatives thanks to the curse—was being taught by the professor he had met at Wyndemere Academy. But Mack?

Why don't I know about my own history? Mack wondered. *Is Jiichan still keeping secrets? Is there something he doesn't want me to know?*

He decided to use this confusion to cement his relationship with Sakura—in her mind, anyway.

"One more thing the old man kept from me," Mack said, making sure to employ the same bitter tone Sakura used when she spoke of his grandfather. "What's hidden in our history that scares him so much that he wouldn't tell me?"

For once Sakura didn't take the opportunity to bash

Mack's grandfather. She was lost in *kitsune* history, like this was a story she had wanted to tell for a long, long time.

"*Kitsune* were favored by Circe, you know, and among Changers alike for our strength and for our regal demeanor. During the *kitsune*'s peak years of power we had more than one thousand bloodlines, strong and fearless *kitsune* in our reach."

"Tell me about them," Mack said. "The bloodlines."

Sakura pointed to the portrait of the four-tailed red fox. "The Roiyaru were known for their brains." Then she moved to stand in front of another portrait. This one was of a striking woman in midtransformation. "The Nozaki, for their beauty."

Sakura stopped in front of a third portrait—one of a fierce-looking, nine-tailed white fox. "One of the bloodlines became known for their battle skills. This bloodline consistently bore the best soldiers, the most powerful *kitsune* known to Changer-kind. Members of this bloodline almost always achieved a *kitsune*'s greatest feat."

"Tails?" Mack asked.

Sakura nodded. "Yes, these *kitsune* consistently earned the maximum number of tails a *kitsune* can attain—nine."

"What was that bloodline called?" Mack asked.

The Shadow Fox pointed to an emblem on the painting. "Chikara," she answered. "They weren't the wealthiest of the bloodlines, or the most elegant, but they were the swiftest and the strongest. The most powerful."

"What happened to them?" Mack asked.

"Hundreds of years ago, a soothsayer prophesized about an ultimate, all-powerful *kitsune*. This particular *kitsune* would be born into the Chikara bloodline, but not know it. The *kitsune* would remain ignorant of the extent of its power."

"That's pretty cool," Mack said. He walked from portrait to portrait, looking for features that might be a mirror of his own. "How do you know which *kitsune* bloodline you come from?" he asked.

He could tell by Sakura's pleased reaction that this was exactly the question she wanted him to ask.

"Bloodline is passed down from family to family, generation to generation," she explained. "Over time, *kitsune* of the Chikara bloodline were threatened, hunted, and killed. No one wanted an all-powerful *kitsune*, no matter how great the *kitsune* helped them become." She stopped to fluff her hair, braided in seven parts to represent her tails, letting that message sink in. "So the Chikara went into hiding. They changed the family name to something more common in Japanese culture, something easily disguised. It was so ordinary that even today, the young *kitsune* of the bloodline don't know—they're still kept in ignorance, locked up, unaware of their true power."

Sakura casually strolled over to another portrait. This one was of two adult *kitsune*. They looked familiar, but Mack couldn't quite figure why. One of them had a tuft of brown fur on its neck—almost like a marking. The marking was one he vaguely recognized, even though Mack was pretty sure he had never seen this particular *kitsune* before.

Something about the tuft of fur triggered memories of a lullaby, and Mack found himself humming it under his breath.

Sakura watched him carefully, a sly gleam in the

corner of her eye. She looked surprised, almost, to see Mack humming—but not *totally* surprised, as if she had expected it.

"The Chikara bloodline," Sakura continued, "hid their young in different corners of the world, scrubbed their bloodline clean of its history, and changed their *notorious*, noble name."

Mack's interest was piqued.

"What did they change their name to?" he asked.

Sakura smiled. It was just the question she'd wanted him to ask.

"They changed their name to Kimura."

Chapter 8
FAMILY SECRETS

Gabriella arrived at the Changer base just as Darren and Ray were finishing their training. She got there at the same time as Yara, the *encantado*, who reported that she had just returned from a mission in the Pacific.

"I met with the leaders of all the finfolk in the Pacific," she reported. "They're ready to do battle with Sakura if she invades the oceans, and they'll do what they can to support us on land."

"What about the *selkies*?" Gabriella asked. "Are they still holding out?"

"We're working on it," Yara said. "In fact, Fiona is with them now. I sensed her presence when I passed the isles underwater. She must be safe with her mother. I'm sure she'll do what she can."

"But that's the worst place for Fiona to be!" Gabriella said. She quickly filled the group in on what Mack had told her the night before. "Oh, why didn't I rush over here last night to warn you right away?" Gabriella said. "Mack told me there's a traitor among the *selkies*. We have to go and get Fiona. She's not safe!"

"We cannot go to the *selkie* isles," Yara said. "It's against our pact with the *selkies*, and we're in the middle of a very delicate negotiation with them. We'll communicate with Fiona when she's back on land."

Gabriella wasn't so sure. "But—"

"She's with her mother," Yara said firmly, cutting her off. "There's nothing we can do now." The older Changer's voice softened when she saw how concerned Gabriella was. "Fiona will be fine. The same magical protections that will keep us away from the *selkie* isles will keep Sakura's forces at bay too."

Ms. Therian was still wincing with each step, so Gabriella put her worries about Fiona aside and did her best to heal the wound some more. It was no use.

Mack's bite would heal, but it would take time.

He definitely wasn't playing games when he attacked Ms. Therian, Gabriella thought. A terrible thought came to her. *Could he be double-crossing us? Maybe he's lying about the surprise attack on the* selkies.

Then Gabriella reminded herself that she was the one who had healed Mack from Sakura's curse. She cast her light-filled, peaceful energy into Mack's mind and let it search for places to heal. The energy moved through Mack, restoring good memory after good memory. The poison of despair and hopelessness left him. Light absorbed the darkness and rendered it helpless.

That was real. That happened. Mack couldn't fake that, Gabriella told herself. Then a small doubt found its way in. *What if he changed back afterward?*

Darren sensed Gabriella's confusion and pulled her aside for a heart-to-heart while the First Four talked about how to use Mack's intel.

"Is everything okay?" Darren asked. "I don't mean to pry, but you seem a little stressed lately."

"This war hasn't brought out the best in me," Gabriella admitted. "I thought being a healer would be really special, but now I can't even heal Ms. Therian. I miss hanging out with my family—with my little sister. I'm worried Mack will get caught by Sakura, and now I'm worried about Fiona, too. I feel totally useless."

"Are you kidding? You did the most valuable thing when you healed Mack," Darren told her. "Now we have a real chance of winning this war and bringing peace to the whole Changer world."

Gabriella felt a little better, but she was still concerned about Fiona. *If the selkies are attacked before we can warn them, and Fiona gets hurt, it'll be all my fault.*

"I just wish . . ." Her voice trailed off.

Darren read her thoughts. "You heard Yara—Fiona will be fine."

"I hope so," Gabriella said with a sigh.

"I wish I had gotten to know you and Mack and Fiona years ago," Darren said. "Before we found out we are Changers. We're a team—a strong team—and we will be for the rest of our lives, but we are friends, too. We all feel down sometimes. Like we're not doing enough or that we're too stressed out to be really useful. That's when we have to prop each other up. We bring out the best in one another."

Darren's words made Gabriella felt a little lighter. "You're right. I'm just tired, I guess."

Darren grinned at her. "The best cure for that is training a new *impundulu* to control his powers," he said, loud enough for Ray to hear.

"As long as he doesn't accidentally cut my hair," Gabriella said sharply. It might look good on Fiona, but she did *not* want to rock short hair at the middle school dance, thank you very much.

"Hey, even Fiona said she looked better than before after that haircut," Ray joked back. "I'm thinking about opening a hair salon when all this is over. I'll call it Lightning Locks."

Darren laughed and shot a lightning arrow at his brother. Ray dodged it neatly.

The First Four headed upstairs and left them to their training. Gabriella changed into her *nahual* form and took off on a run.

Catch me if you can, bird boy, she communicated to Ray telepathically. She was so fast that all he saw was a blur.

Ray transformed, spreading his wings, and took off after her.

The three of them flew, pounced, shot arrows, and basically pummeled one another for the next hour until they were all slumped on the floor, giggling.

All that exercise made me feel better, Gabriella realized. *Going to battle is fun when you know that no one's going to get hurt.*

"Something weird happened before you got here, by the way," Darren told Gabriella when they had caught their breath. "I don't really know how to explain it. Mr. Kimura brought out some pancakes and—"

"So weird," Gabriella laughed.

Darren smirked.

"He mentioned something about Mack's mother. It was almost like—almost like she knew she was going to die."

"She passed on the pancakes recipe before that could happen," Ray added.

"Maybe he meant when she was old. We all know we'll die someday, right?" Gabriella said.

"No," Darren answered. "This was like she knew she was going to die *soon* and was taking care of things."

"But she died in a car crash, didn't she?" Gabriella

asked. "With Mack's dad. No one can predict they're going to die in an accident like that."

"That's the story, but I'm beginning to wonder if there is more to it," Darren said. "Something about what Mr. Kimura said didn't fit."

"Well, I know what Fiona would say, and I think right now, I agree with her. Let's check *The Compendium*," Gabriella said.

"What's that?" Ray asked.

Gabriella walked over to a nook in the Changer base and pulled out a very old book. "*The Compendium* is a precious resource for Changers. It's a living book. It contains our Changer history. All our history—maps, relics, family trees, secrets."

"It's a magical book," Darren added. "Fiona found it in the New Brighton University Library when we were being chased by evil warlocks."

Ray did a double take, as if to ask *Evil warlocks?*, but didn't interrupt.

He's still getting used to all this Changer stuff, Gabriella thought. And then she felt sad again. Would she ever get to introduce Maritza to this world? Would she ever want to?

"The book decides who can read it, not the other way around," Darren continued. "It reveals its secrets only to the right people at the right time."

"How do we know we're the right people?" Ray asked.

"The book will tell us," Gabriella answered. She placed her hands on the book's leather cover and took a deep breath. "Today we want to find out about Makoto Kimura and his parents. Most importantly, we want to find out how his parents died."

She raised her hands. As the three of them watched the book's cover creak open, its tissue-thin pages began to flutter and then turn.

Gabriella remembered how amazed she was the first time she saw the book do this. Today she saw that amazement mirrored in Ray's face.

Slowly, the book settled down and rested open on the right pages. The letters and words appeared to be in an ancient and indecipherable language.

"I guess it doesn't want us to know what happened," Ray said.

But before the words were out of his mouth, the letters and words on the page began to rearrange themselves. In seconds they were clear and legible.

"What's this?" Darren asked.

"It's all about the *kitsune* bloodlines," Gabriella said. "'*Kitsune* were among the very first Changers,'" she read. She skimmed the rest of the passage, sharing the highlights with Darren and Ray, and then she moved on to a passage about the most powerful bloodline of all.

"'The members of the bloodline, the Chikara bloodline, became known for their skill in battle. It consistently bore the best soldiers, the most powerful *kitsune* known to Changer-kind. Members of this bloodline almost always achieved a *kitsune*'s greatest feat—earning all nine tails.

"'Hundreds of years ago, a soothsayer prophesized about an ultimate, all-powerful *kitsune*,'" Gabriella continued. "'This particular *kitsune* would be born into the Chikara bloodline, but he or she would not know it. They would remain ignorant of the extent of their power.'"

"Wow," Darren said. "Do you think this could have something to do with Sakura? She started this war because she wants to destroy Mr. Kimura. Could one of them be this all-powerful *kitsune*?"

"From what you've told me, that's what Sakura wants to be—all-powerful," Ray said. "If she wins this war, do you think she'll become the all-powerful one?"

Gabriella scanned the rest of the page, looking for answers.

"'Today there are only three known living *kitsune* of the Chikara bloodline,'" Gabriella read. "'Akira Kimura, helm of the First Four, passed the bloodline down to his deceased son, Shiro Kimura. Shiro passed this bloodline down to his own son, Makoto, of Willow Cove.'"

She eyed Darren and Ray to make sure they understood exactly what she was saying—that Mack was the all-powerful *kitsune*, and he did not know that.

"'There is another *kitsune* of the Chikara lineage, however,'" Gabriella continued. "'A female, orphaned at a young age, who is a distant relative of Akira Kimura's, as well as a former student of his.'" Gabriella paused, her voice rising as she realized the importance of what she was saying. "'This *kitsune*, as some call her, is named Sakura Hiyamoto.'"

She looked up at Darren and Ray, her eyes wide. There was complete silence for a moment.

"Sakura? Like, Sakura, Shadow Fox Sakura? Like the one you're at war with?" Ray asked.

Gabriella nodded, too stunned to speak.

"If Sakura knows who Mack really is, then maybe this whole thing is a plot," Darren said.

"A plot?" Ray asked.

"If she wins the war and destroys the First Four, the only thing that stands between her and being all-powerful is Mack. Maybe she plans to use him to help her win."

"And then kill him," Gabriella said, finishing his thought.

"Dude," Ray said. "We've got to ask Mack's grandfather about this."

Chapter 9
THE SKINWALKERS

Fiona waited nervously outside the cave where the *selkies'* Council of Elders met. The last time she had attended a council meeting, things hadn't gone so well. Now her mother wanted her to sit in again. However, she would have been much happier—and a lot more welcome—hanging out with Aiyana.

Leana put her hands on Fiona's shoulders and looked her in the eye. "You're my daughter and their princess, but you still need to show them that you're one of us. It's your royal duty to win them over. That's the only way we can come together with the rest of the Changers to defeat Sakura."

That's too heavy a burden to place on my shoulders, Fiona thought. *What if I fail?*

Leana sensed her daughter's doubts. "Show them who you are in your heart, and you'll be successful. You're a natural leader. I have every confidence in your ability to win them over."

Fiona took a deep breath. "I'll do my best," she said.

Leana smiled and gave her a hug. "I know you will."

The queen adjusted her tiara, drew her *selkie* cloak around her shoulders, and entered the cave. The walls were lit with glowing conch shells and burning torches. A huge driftwood table sat in the center of the chamber. The torches seemed to flare brighter when the council members rose and bowed to their queen, though that might have been a trick of the light.

"Your Majesty," the members murmured.

Leana sat in her throne at the head of the table. It was only then that Fiona saw the smaller, intricately carved, driftwood throne that sat next to her mother's. The delicate pictures seemed to tell the whole of *selkie* history, and Fiona couldn't wait to study them at leisure. Beautiful pink shells and pieces of coral covered the throne's back and the arms, making it a living thing. Fiona sat in it and felt both the weight and the grandeur of *selkie* history move through her. For the very first time, she felt like a princess—and a future queen.

The last time Fiona had attended a council meeting, her presence had been a surprise, and she sat in a makeshift chair drawn to a corner of the table at the last minute. It had made her feel unwelcome. Today the council had prepared for her presence with this beautiful throne. She nodded her thanks.

They're trying to make me one of them, Fiona thought. *Maybe Mom's right. If I show them who I am in my heart, they'll come to see I am one of them.*

She sat quietly as the meeting began. The ritual was familiar from the last time she had been in this chamber.

"Children of the sea, we gather here tonight as a council of *selkies*," Leana said. Her voice was soft yet demanded control. "May the moon pull us to the correct conclusions; may the wind whisper wisdom in our ears; may the tides turn our hearts to justice in all matters that come before this council—tonight and for all time."

"May it be," Fiona and the other *selkies* chorused in unison.

"The timepiece," Mom said, holding her hand in the air.

A young *selkie* scurried forward, carrying an elaborate hourglass filled with pure-white sand. Leana took it, turned it upside down, and glanced at a piece of parchment before her—the list of matters that would be addressed that evening.

A *selkie* named Maeve reported on a dispute between the *selkies* who lived off the western Irish coast and the land-based Changers who had taken over an unused island nearby.

Fiona asked a pertinent question about the treaty that granted the *selkies* this land, winning admiring looks from at least half of the members of the council, including her mother. She also weighed in on a decision her mom made about a dispute between the finfolk in the Southern Ocean and the *selkies* who ruled that part of the sea.

I'm winning them over, Fiona thought. *They're beginning to see that I'm one of them and I have something to contribute!*

There was one *selkie*, however, whose face seemed

to turn to stone every time she looked at Fiona. Erynn was the wizened old *selkie* whose disapproval and ridicule made the last council meeting so difficult for Fiona.

Fiona caught the old woman's glance now, and Erynn narrowed her eyes and pursed her lips in disapproval.

When Leana asked if there was any more business to attend to, Fiona rose to her feet before Erynn could do anything to stop her. "I think we must address the issue of the Shadow Fox and her war with the Changers," she said, her heart hammering in her chest. "And how we can support them."

Erynn's disapproval and derision were swift. "That's not our fight," she sneered. "The First Four want our help, yet they offer nothing in return."

"The First Four are fighting right now for our freedom—for the freedom of all Changer-kind, including the *selkies*," Fiona said. "If the Shadow Fox gets her way, we'll all be her puppets."

Erynn's eyes flashed with surprise at the word "puppets," confirming what Fiona had suspected—Erynn was the one who told the other *selkie*s that Fiona was a puppet of the First Four.

Fiona pressed on. "If Sakura defeats the First Four, she will turn on us next. No one is safe while the Shadow Fox is loose in the world. We'll be enslaved to her evil power. We have to stand up and fight. We must do something now before it's too late."

She noticed that some around the table were listening intently, but Erynn and a few others were even more intent on undermining her message.

"It's the First Four who want to see us enslaved," Erynn spat. "They want to steal our magic for their own ends. As they always have."

"The princess is exaggerating about Sakura," a man yelled. "Why, I heard even Akira Kimura's grandson joined her forces! How bad can she be? Isn't it about time that all the Changers followed our lead and threw off the yoke of the First Four?"

Fiona and Leana both tried to jump into the conversation, to speak reason, but the forces against them were too loud and persistent.

"You're pretty, but oh so very young," Erynn said with

a snide smile. She turned to address the table. "I heard her earlier. She couldn't even master a simple song."

A chorus of "A simple song?" echoed around the room. Fiona's eyes flashed with anger, but she bit her lip. Her mother had told her that the Amhrán Sinsear was nearly impossible for most *selkies* to perform. Erynn was being completely unfair, but fairness didn't serve the elder *selkie*'s ends—not when it came to Fiona.

"Silence," Leana said, her voice filling the chamber. Suddenly, she had a queenly command of the room. "We must have a reasoned discussion and cannot do that if we're all talking over one another. I will listen to what you have to say, one *selkie* at a time, and only then will I make a decision."

Erynn muttered something under her breath, something about Leana not having any subjects to follow her if she made the wrong decision.

"I said silence," Leana commanded again.

There were murmurs of "Yes, my Queen," but Fiona noticed that Erynn did not murmur those words.

Leana turned over the hourglass. "I will hear you one at a time," she said.

Erynn glared at Fiona. "I believe you have ears only for your daughter—your daughter who knows almost nothing of our *selkie* world."

"One at a time," Leana repeated.

Erynn backed down under Leana's harsh glare, but Fiona knew it was just a matter of time before she started attacking again.

Many of the council members who spoke believed the First Four were being too dramatic. They said that Sakura didn't pose any real threat. Fiona knew that wasn't true.

How can I convince them? she thought. *How can I show them Sakura is the evil one?*

She tried to listen calmly while the council members bashed her for being young, for being overly dramatic, for being ignorant. All the while Fiona hoped the perfect argument would come to her, one that would turn everyone around—even Erynn. This was too important to mess up.

If I ever need luck, it's right now, Fiona thought. *Luck o' the Irish.* She began to sing the Amhrán Sinsear under her breath. Then, for added measure, she added the Gaelic verse she had learned from Aiyana.

I don't know what the Gaelic words mean, but I will take all the help I can get. C'mon Murphy clan, I need you.

Fiona had just begun the Gaelic verse when a huge purple cloud suddenly filled the chamber and Fiona heard hooves.

Hooves? In the selkie isles? That doesn't make sense. The isles are protected from humans and Changers alike with selkie magic.

What could possibly have hooves here?

Fiona looked up. She gasped! An army of *selkies* and other finfolk were about to spring out of the cloud, ready to attack. But these were not like any *selkies* Fiona had ever seen before. These *selkies* had hooves and armor. There were shouts of "In the name of Shadow Fox!" coming from their midst, leaving no doubt about it—these were members of Sakura's evil forces.

"Skinwalkers!" one of the council members yelled.

There was a gasp around the table. "How was our *selkie* protection jeopardized?" Erynn yelled. "Who has betrayed us?"

A figure broke out of the purple cloud, and now it

was Fiona's turn to gasp. The figure was Aiyana. *Aiyana?* *Aiyana* was on Sakura's side?

Aiyana smiled broadly at everyone around the table. "Bonjour!" She laughed, pointing at Fiona. "Blame *her* for breaking your precious protection. *She* performed dark magic—*she* performed the dark verse of the Amhrán Sinsear. Your princess broke your own protection curse. You wouldn't join us while you had the chance. And now you'll pay. Sakura and her kingdom will rise, and she'll show no mercy to those weakling *selkies* who did not support her."

Aiyana and a few other skinwalkers grabbed Fiona and her mother.

"Mom!" Fiona yelled. "What did I do?"

Her mother's face was drawn and tight. She was singling quietly—trying to find the magic to halt the attack. But while Fiona watched, one of the skinwalkers used dark magic to bind her mother's lips closed and stop her song.

Fiona turned to the others at the table. "I didn't know! I didn't know!"

Before anyone could answer, Aiyana threw off her

selkie cloak to reveal she was really a *tengu*—or wearing the pelt of a *tengu*, at least. A skinwalker jumped in and bound Fiona's mouth too, so she couldn't speak. As a *tengu*, Aiyana held Fiona and her mother, ready to take them somewhere else. Fiona felt the familiar whoosh and then a sharp jolt before she was transported far away from the one place her mother had assured her would always be safe.

Chapter 10
THE DOUBLE AGENT

"Kimura," Mack said, gazing up at the portrait of the two adult kitsune. He tried to keep his voice calm. "That means—"

"Yes," Sakura snapped, cutting him off. "You're the *kitsune* from the prophecy—the one all-powerful *kitsune*. Thanks to me, we will unlock your power, together."

Although her words were sweet as candy, Mack could hear the underlying bitterness in her voice. That's what she had meant when she'd shouted at his grandfather in New York City. Sakura thought that she was the chosen one. But she wasn't. It was Mack. It was Mack all along.

Sakura confirmed what Mack had already guessed.

"I, too, am from the Chikara bloodline," she said. "I will train you in ways your grandfather never could. He's afraid of your power. I am not. Together, you and I will rule all Changer-kind."

Mack nodded, breathless and too overwhelmed for words.

Does she really want us to rule together? Or does she want to use my power to win the war? Is she planning to get rid of me when it's all over?

The more Mack thought about it, the more obvious it seemed. Sakura had thought she was the chosen *kitsune*—until Mack arrived.

Mack still wanted to know why the *kitsune* in the portrait—the one of the marking on her neck—looked familiar. Why did it draw this lullaby out of him and this feeling of warmth and comfort?

Mack was still trying to decide how to word his questions when one of Sakura's minions arrived by *tengu*. He said he had a message, and the Shadow Fox stepped away.

As she did, Mack continued to study the portrait. There was something just at the edge of his mind—a memory, maybe—but he couldn't call it up. The memory—if it was real at all—was too elusive.

Sakura was back much too quickly for Mack to sort anything out. Her mood had lifted. The bitterness of a moment before was replaced with excitement. "I have very good news," she told Mack. "We've captured one of your little friends. We must go."

"'Little friends'?" Mack asked, carefully controlling his voice. "Which one of them was foolish enough to fall into your hands, Master?"

Though what Mack *really* wanted to ask was, IS MY FRIEND OKAY?

"That's not important," Sakura said. "What is important is the fact that the rest of them, along with the First Four, will try to rescue her, and we'll be waiting. This may very well be the last battle we have to fight before establishing our rule."

Her? Sakura said "her," Mack realized. That means Gabriella or Fiona. It's hard to believe that either one of them would leave the magical protection that the First Four established all around them. What could have happened? Did it have something to do with the attack on the selkies that Sakura had planned? Or something else?

"Are you ready to take over the world, my apprentice?" Sakura continued. "Because I am, and I'm bringing you with me."

Mack bowed low, trying to hide his solemn eyes. He kept his breathing steady to hide the panic rushing through him.

"I'm ready, Master. Thank you, Master," he said. His voice squeaked at the end, but he was glad she didn't notice.

Mack's hand was shaking when the *tengu* indicated that he was ready to transport them.

"I know you're excited," Sakura said. "We've been waiting for this for a long time. Keep your wits about you and concentrate on taking out one of them at a time. All will be well."

Mack felt a whoosh, and seconds later found himself in the middle of a Changer fortress in Central Park in New York City. His eyes widened when he saw Fiona and Leana. Fiona looked different—her hair was chopped off, but he could tell she tried to disguise it with magic; any human would see it as long. Yet this was the least important thing about her. Magical chains were wrapped around Fiona's and her mother's hands and legs, and their mouths were bound—so that they couldn't sing.

They can't sing, he realized. *Without their voices, they have no magic. They're powerless!*

A skinwalker named Aiyana bowed to Sakura as they walked toward the prisoners.

"The skinwalkers would like to present a gift to you, Sakura," she said. "We hope you accept this gift as a pledge from us to your rule."

Sakura smirked and circled the two *selkies*. "My, such a pretty little gift," she said with a sneer.

Mack tried to hide how truly terrified he was.

He had to hold himself back from running to his friend and freeing her. *I have to be very careful if Fiona's going to have any chance at all.*

He raked his eyes over his friend and her mother. "What a welcome sight," he said, matching Sakura's tone. "Fiona always did talk too much." He turned toward Sakura and forced himself to smile. "Another chink in the First Four's armor."

"The skinwalkers are attacking the *selkies* at this very moment," Aiyana said to Sakura, who was positively delighted by the news. "Those who don't pledge their allegiance to you will soon be disposed of."

Disposed of? What does that mean? Mack wondered. He wished he could tell Fiona and her mother that he'd do what he could for them, but with Sakura watching, that was impossible. His eyes danced from one of Sakura's soldiers to another, all proudly standing around the prisoners.

How am I going to rescue Fiona and her mother?

Sakura smirked. "Not so very queenly now, are you?" she said to Leana. "You should have joined me when you had the chance. I might have let the *selkies* continue to rule themselves. It's too late for that now. Your subjects are no longer yours—they are *mine* to do with what I wish. Perhaps I'll take their cloaks, so they can no longer transform. I think my pet skinwalkers would love some *selkie* cloaks, wouldn't you, my sweets?"

Aiyana and her minions cackled.

Mack knew that for a *selkie* to lose his or her cloak was the absolute worst thing that could happen. It was a cruel threat, even for Sakura.

Mack could see Fiona's eyes flash with anger, and Sakura laughed, noticing it too.

"The rest of my forces will be here in two hours' time," Sakura said. "And then the final battle will begin. The First Four will be eliminated once and for all." She turned to Mack. "My apprentice and I will soon have control of the entire Changer world."

Mack raised his chin and once again forced himself to smile. "A gloriously evil new world," he said. Then he walked to the edge of the fortress, a giant magical tent, to get away from Sakura's eyes. He could see humans walking back and forth, avoiding the invisible boundaries without knowing why. They had no idea of the danger right under their noses.

Changers have always protected humans, but Sakura has no interest in that, Mack thought. He and a few of her followers had demanded they protect the battlegrounds before, but what would happen later? *One by one she'll take away the humans' rights and comforts until they're little more than slaves—just like the magical beings in her grip.* He thought of his friend, Joel Hastings. It was a horrible thought to think of Joel enslaved.

Mack put those thoughts out of his head while he tried to come up with a plan to help Fiona and the First Four.

A short while later, while the *selkies* were incapacitated and Sakura prepared for war, Sakura called him over to join her. They still had an hour or so left before the rest of the forces got there.

"We need to fortify ourselves for the coming battle," Sakura said to Mack. "Come, apprentice. Join me for some tea."

How strange that her rituals are so much like Jiichan's, he thought. That must be because Grandfather trained her. She held on to his customs, if not his goodness.

Slowly, an idea dawned. Mack drank cup after cup of tea until he could barely take another sip. "Excuse me, Master," he said, getting to his feet. "I need to find a bathroom. I'll be back long before the battle begins."

Sakura nodded absently. She was busy getting updates on the *selkie* battle.

Mack ran out of the park to Fifth Avenue, casting around for a bathroom. Of course, it was New York, so there were no *free* bathrooms for use. He found a coffee shop and bought a cake pop so that they would let him use the bathroom. He was on his way out of the bathroom, hoping to get someone to loan him a cell phone, when he spotted an old-fashioned phone booth. Sakura had taken his cell phone away so that the First Four couldn't use it to track him, but he could call them on this thing. He slipped into the phone booth, dropped as many quarters as he had into the coin slot, and dialed Gabriella's number.

Pick up! Pick up! he thought desperately. *Please. Please don't go to voicemail.*

Chapter 11
THE FINAL BATTLE

Gabriella's cell phone chirped, and she checked the screen. It was a New York City number. One she didn't recognize.

"Hello?"

"Gabriella!" Mack yelled.

"It's Mack!" she told Darren and Ray. She put the phone on speaker, and they all gathered around.

"I only have a minute before Sakura begins to suspect why I'm gone," he said. "Sakura's got a fortress in Central Park, in the same spot where we had our last battle here. Fiona and Leana are both prisoners—she's bound their mouths so they don't have magic. Skinwalkers are fighting the *selkies* right now. As soon as the battle for the *selkie* isles is over, Sakura's entire army will come here for what she calls the final battle."

Gabriella started to ask a question, but Mack cut her off.

"I've got to go," he said. "Get here. Hurry!"

Gabriella raced upstairs to let the First Four know what Mack had told her. Darren and Ray were on her heels.

"We've got to get to New York and save Fiona," Gabriella said. "Now!"

She paced back and forth while the First Four considered what to do. *Hurry, hurry, hurry!* she chanted in her head.

Ms. Therian wanted to travel to New York immediately and take on Sakura. "Now, before her army is at full strength."

"*You're* not at full strength. Your leg is still healing," Yara told her.

"And what if this is a trick to get us to leave this Changer base unprotected?" Sefu added.

"Yes, we must consider the possibility that this is a trick," Mr. Kimura said.

"Mack wouldn't trick us," Gabriella said. "I know he wouldn't."

"No, I don't believe Makoto is trying to trick us," Mr. Kimura said. "But he may not know the full story. If anyone one in Sakura's camp still suspects him, this could be a test. He could be directing us right into a trap."

Gabriella protested, "But he said that Sakura's entire army was on its way. And Fiona—"

"We'll do everything to save Fiona," Mr. Kimura said, "and to win this battle. But we can't leave this base unprotected. It's one of our last strongholds—still protected from Sakura's magic. We'll leave some forces behind to protect it and call the younglings and the elderly here—all those who are unable to fight."

"Dorina, you must stay here with Yara and Sefu," he continued. "I will lead our army in New York."

Ms. Therian reluctantly agreed. Her leg still wasn't at its full strength. "Hurry home, Akira. *With* Fiona and Makoto."

Mr. Kimura held his old friend in his gaze for a minute. Gabriella could see the trust and the love they had for each other—just like the trust and love she had for her friends.

Gabriella and Darren were anxious to go, but had to wait for Mr. Kimura to contact the entire Changer world and ask them to go to New York City. Younglings began streaming toward the base for safety from around the globe.

"Wow," Ray whispered. "There are a lot of you."

"A lot of *us*," Darren corrected.

"Maybe you should stay behind with Ms. Therian," Gabriella said. "The fight will be hard, and you still have a lot of training to do."

"Absolutely not," Ray said. "If this is Darren's fight, it's my fight too."

Darren put a hand on his brother's arm. "Follow my lead. And be careful."

"You got it, Birdbrain Number Two," Ray said, looking around. "How are we going to get to New York?" he asked. "Do you have your own airplane? I'm not sure my wings are up to a cross-country flight."

"We've got something much, much better," Darren said with a smile.

A second later Margaery arrived, and they gave Ray a quick introduction to traveling by *tengu*. Mr. Kimura,

Darren, Gabriella, and Ray each put a hand on her arm, and the next thing they knew they were standing in the middle of Central Park. A squirrel dropped the acorn it was holding when it saw them, but enchantments kept them from the humans' eyes.

Supporters of the First Four were streaming in. The minute they entered Sakura's stronghold, Gabriella could see how outnumbered the followers of the First Four were. Sakura's forces had tripled since their last battle.

She spotted Fiona and Leana in chains in the center of the fortress. "Fiona!" Gabriella yelled. She transformed to bound over and free them. But before she could do anything to help her friend, a skinwalker wearing a *nahual* pelt came at her. The two *nahuals* circled each other, snarling, but Gabriella was clearly the stronger of the two.

The skinwalker came at her anyway, and Gabriella easily swatted it away. It tried to run in the other direction, but Gabriella pounced on it in one leap and completely took charge. Unconscious, the skinwalker transformed back into a weak-looking man. She signaled for an *aatxe* to come and place magical chains on the creature and then turned on her heels toward Fiona.

Each time Gabriella tried to take a step toward Fiona, she was attacked by another Changer and then another. Some were skinwalkers; others took different Changer forms. Each time she knocked one of them out, another appeared. She could feel herself beginning to tire.

A giant snakelike creature with the head and tusks of an elephant, a *grootslang*, slithered through the grass toward her. It rose up to squeeze her in a death grip. Gabriella turned on it with a hiss, but her energy was fading. Ray, spotting her trouble from a few feet a way, quickly took care of a gargoyle with a bolt of lighting and then came to her aid.

"Great control!" Gabriella yelled, watching him slice the *grootslang* in two with a fire arrow.

It was only then that Gabriella noticed that Darren had cast a force field around Fiona and Leana so that Sakura's forces couldn't harm them. But he was so busy deflecting her soldiers that he couldn't free them either.

She and Ray fought their way over to Darren. The three of them stood in a tight circle, their backs to one another, fighting off anything that came near.

Gabriella could see that Sakura and Mack were squared off against Mr. Kimura. *They found him,* she thought. *Or maybe he found them.*

The battle waged around them, but the three of them weren't moving. They weren't fighting with brute force as the others were. They were having a war of words. With her powerful *nahual* ears, Gabriella could tune into their conversation, even from a distance.

"Sakura, it didn't have to be this way," Mr. Kimura said. "If you hadn't killed my son—"

Gabriella's fur stood up straight. It made sense. All the secrets. *That* was what this was all about. Sakura had *killed Mr. Kimura's son.*

His words were cut off by a powerful, anguished cry.

"What did you say?" Mack bellowed. "Your son—my father?"

Mr. Kimura turned to Mack. Everything about his demeanor—his facial expression, his posture—was etched with sadness. It was clear this was a powerful secret, revealed at last.

"Sakura—the Shadow Fox—killed your mother and

father," he admitted. "Your mother spent many years tracking Sakura. She wanted to bind her powers and protect you."

"You told me they died in an accident!" Mack yelled. "Why?"

"That's what I told the world," Mr. Kimura said. "It was *Sakura* who destroyed the rest of the Chikara bloodline in the hopes that she would be the powerful *kitsune* the soothsayer prophesied, not another *kitsune*. I needed to keep your existence a secret. I wanted to protect you from her as long as I could. But when you defeated Auden Ironbound, the whole Changer world learned of you—and your power. I couldn't keep you hidden anymore."

Mack turned on Sakura. Gabriella could see he was struggling, but it was too soon in the battle for him to reveal his true allegiance.

Stay on Sakura's side, she communicated to Mack. *Or we won't win.*

She killed my parents! Mack communicated back.

Gabriella had to calm Mack down. She quickly entered into a meditative state and spirit-walked into

Mack's mind. His thoughts were frantic and jumbled. Gabriella could feel all of Mack's feelings, to the point she wasn't sure what belonged to whom.

Suddenly, Mack understood why he recognized the portrait in Japan of the two *kitsune*. It was his mother and father. Right before she killed them. His mother, Mari—her *kitsune* markings were like the freckles on her skin. He remembered that now. And the lullaby. She used to sing that lullaby.

Mack was filled with a passionate rage.

I'll kill her—I'll kill the Shadow Fox! he thought.

"Mack, it's me. I know you want revenge for your parents. But you've got to fight this fear and this rage for a little while longer. Don't let Sakura see that you've turned against her. We may need you still," Gabriella said as she spirit-walked.

Gabriella was so focused on Mack's thoughts that she let her guard down. Outside of the spirit realm and in the physical one, a *mo'o*, a Hawaiian water dragon, charged at her. Gabriella found herself flying backward—for real. Not only was she booted from Mack's mind and hit her head on a tree, the *mo'o* was able to seriously injure two of Gabriella's paws. They were scraped raw.

Darren, in his *impundulu* form, swooped in and gently picked her up with his talons. The next thing Gabriella knew, she was sitting on the sidelines.

Great, Gabriella thought. *I come out here to fight, and I'm rerouted to the sides. Some great fighter I am, right?*

Chapter 12
THE CHIKARA BLOODLINE

Darren brought Gabriella to the outskirts of the battle. He was confident her wounds weren't life-threatening, but he didn't think she'd be fighting anymore that day. She needed to rest.

I feel so useless, Gabriella told him.

You're not useless, Darren communicated back. *You took out, like, six of Sakura's forces, and you helped Mack stay calm. That's incredible, Gabriella. You're incredible. Now stay here and take it easy.*

Thankfully, Gabriella's grandmother and her tía Rosa had just arrived to work on healing the injured warriors. Darren knew she'd be safe with them. He passed her on to their care and sped back into the fray.

More good news. Sakura's troops seemed to be shrinking, and supporters of the First Four were pouring into the fortress. Darren was surprised to see a significant number of *selkies* arrive with them.

The skinwalkers must have failed. The selkies won the battle! Sakura's going to be furious, thought Darren.

The *selkies* weren't able to transform because they weren't in the water, but they had come to do whatever they could for their queen and for their princess. Darren was impressed by how much they could do in their human forms. *Selkies* typically didn't spend a lot of time out of the water, but it was like they were skilled martial artists, ready for anything.

While he watched, one of the *selkies* drenched one of Sakura's *grootslangs* with a water shield, much like the one Fiona had used with Ray only days earlier. Had it been only days earlier? It felt like a lifetime ago. The water hit the *grootslang* right in the face. It was a critical hit.

Other *selkies* formed a circle around Fiona and her mother and began to sing.

I hope that's a song that will release them, Darren

thought. *How terrible it must be to have your mouth bound when your magic is in your song.*

Darren, however, had too much on his plate to watch the *selkies* for long. He shot a fire arrow at a *nykur* that was descending on the *selkie* circle. The *nykur* doused it with a wave of river water, but it wasn't aware of Ray on its other side. While Darren continued to draw the *nykur's* attention, Ray circled behind him and cast some fire arrows of his own.

That's my birdbrain bro, Darren thought.

Fighting alongside Ray was different from fighting alongside Fiona, Mack, or Gabriella. Darren felt in tune with his brother. It was almost like when they were little, arguing for their dad to take them for root beer floats after school. They nodded to one another. Then the brothers stood back-to-back, taking on all of Sakura's forces in the vicinity. Ray was doing an amazing job, especially considering this was his first battle.

"You're doing great," Darren said.

Ray laughed. "It's kind of like engineering," he answered. "It's figuring out how things work, and—in this case—how to break them."

"So you chose the right thing to major in in college," Darren said.

Ray's ease and self-assurance sent a wave of confidence through Darren. Ray raised his talons and managed to sideline ten of Sakura's skinwalkers with one blow. They were cast aside but wouldn't be permanently hurt.

But Fiona and her mother were still bound. Whatever dark magic Sakura's forces had used was holding up well against the *selkies'* collective song. Yet all hope was not lost. Darren looked around and noticed . . . only the Shadow Fox was still standing now.

Sakura, however, was so intent on her argument with Mr. Kimura that she didn't seem to realize what was happening around her.

Does she even know she's losing? Darren wondered. He couldn't tell.

Supporters of the First Four were all around— transporting Sakura's soldiers to prison and healing the wounded.

Darren and Ray, who had both taken to flying low in the sky, descended near Mack and transformed into their human forms. They could listen in on everything now. They bent their heads closer.

Sakura and Mr. Kimura were in a standoff, fighting with words instead of force. Mack stood at Sakura's side. Darren could feel waves of anger coming off him—and off Sakura. Mr. Kimura was, as always, unruffled, but Darren sensed a great sadness in him too. The last time Darren felt this kind of unease, his parents announced they were getting a divorce.

"You made me believe I was the Chikara *kitsune* in the prophecy. The all-powerful one," Sakura spat at Mr. Kimura. "You pushed and pushed to turn me into that *kitsune*. You placed it above everything. Above my safety. Even above yours. *You* wanted to be known as the trainer to the greatest *kitsune* who ever lived. Everything I am, I am because you forced me to be. This is your fault."

"I did push you too far, Sakura," Mr. Kimura admitted. "I was young and ambitious. It is one of the great sorrows of my life. My greatest mistake."

Sakura waved his words aside. "You wanted me for the glory I could bring you. And then you had a son, Shiro, and suddenly, he was more important than me. Your attachment for your son shut me out."

Wow, Darren thought, *is this all about jealousy? Was Sakura jealous of Mack's dad?*

"I tried to include you, but your envy and possessiveness got in the way," Mr. Kimura said. "And your lust for power."

"That's right!" Sakura yelled. "I wanted the power you promised to me. But how could I be the most powerful Chikara when you started training your own son, too? When you had us practice with each other? I could not. I had to do something else. So I hunted down every *kitsune* of our bloodline and killed them."

"That's when you disappeared," Mr. Kimura said. "That's when you became the Shadow Fox."

"To take *my* power for myself," Sakura said. "I wasn't going to let you hand it over to a weakling like Shiro without a fight."

"But that's not how power is bestowed," Mr. Kimura said. "It's not me who decides who gets it. And real power, true power, isn't *taken* by means of threats and intimidation. True power comes from within—from wanting the best for the beings around you—even more than you want it for yourself."

Sakura scoffed. "I killed every last one of them. Most of them I made to look like accidents so that you wouldn't figure out what I was doing. It's easy to hide when you live in the shadows. And then only Shiro was left. I planned to kill him last, to punish you by making sure you knew exactly what I was doing and why. But his wife, Mari, got in the way."

For the first time since Darren joined the small group, he saw Mack react. He seemed to deflate for a second, and then he rose up to his full height. It was as if he grew three inches in one breath.

"*You* killed my mother," he said, snarling.

Sakura's eyes raked over Mack. There was a look of surprise in them.

Did she really think Mack was on her side until right now? Darren wondered. *Whoa. Mack's cloaking must be super impressive.* He was suddenly really proud of his good friend and made a mental note to buy him a pizza when this was all over.

"Your mother found out about my plan some-how," Sakura said. "She wasn't Chikara; she was from a *lesser* bloodline, one whose name I know not, but she discovered that I was missing and that all the members of the Chikara bloodline were dying one by one, and she put everything together. She knew her husband and young son were in danger."

"She tried to save us, didn't she?" Mack asked.

"She did—she tracked me down and challenged me, but her weakling power was no match for mine. I ate her memories. I tortured her unconsciously into telling me where my former trainer and his son were living, and then I delivered a killing blow. She was foolish. She need not have died. Your father was next," she said to Mack.

A shiver ran up Darren's spine. *She says it so matter-of-factly, like taking a life is nothing.*

"Unfortunately, I didn't know about *you*," Sakura said to Mack. "Neither of your parents gave up *that* piece of information. Confident that I had destroyed any *kitsune* who might challenge my power, I chose to go underground and bide my time before I took over the Changer world."

"So what happened?" Mack asked.

"*You* happened. I heard about your fight with Auden Ironbound. The Changer world was buzzing with news about the youngling *kitsune* who had defeated the powerful warlock and saved the Changer world. And I needed to know more."

"So you weren't the most powerful *kitsune* after all?" Mack asked.

Sakura's eyes flashed with fury.

"No, it was you. And then I knew. The only way to claim my title as the most powerful *kitsune* of the Chikara bloodline was to kill you."

"But you haven't," Mack said, confused. "You could have killed me a hundred times, and you didn't."

"No. Not *yet*. I wanted to play with you first. I liked the idea of torturing your grandfather by making you *mine*," she said. Anger shimmered in the air around her. Darren could sense it.

Darren had heard enough. He didn't think Sakura would ever give up the fight. Mack and his grandfather and all of the Changer world would always be in danger if they didn't find a permanent way to silence her.

He turned to Ray. "We're not killers; we're not Sakura. But what if you cursed her instead? The professor said that's your special power."

"I don't think I could ever do that. I remember how it felt to be cursed. To feel deep inside that something was wrong and not to be able to fix it—or even know what it was," Ray said. "I don't think it's right."

"But we're talking about a killer here," Darren said. He eyed Sakura—she was still staring at Mack and his grandfather with a look of intense rage. She didn't seem to have ears or eyes for anyone else.

The only thing holding her back from performing more dark magic is the fact that she's surrounded by First Four supporters, Darren thought.

"Mack will never be safe from her," Darren said. "None of us will."

"It's still not right," Ray said. "Besides, won't it affect others in her bloodline? Will I be cursing Mack and his grandfather, too?"

Darren didn't have an answer to that. Ray was right. Given his ability to curse an entire bloodline, cursing Sakura could have much larger consequences than sidelining the Shadow Fox. But what else could they do? They couldn't kill her.

Just then, he heard a cry from across the battlefield.

"Wait! I have an idea."

Darren looked over and saw Esi Akosua limping her way toward him. "Esi! You're injured."

"Esi?" Ray asked. "As in the *anansi* who broke the curse?"

Darren nodded, grinning.

Ray whistled.

"She is beautiful," Ray said. He looked at Darren. "And you're blushing. Got a little crush, Birdbrain Number Two?"

Darren gave Ray a look that silenced him.

"I'm okay," Esi said, once she'd finally ambled over. "The healers are working on the more serious wounds right now. But I'll be fine once they get around to me." She turned to Ray. "I heard you talk about curses, and I'm here for this. There's a way to curse just Sakura instead of her entire bloodline. That's really the best way to deal with someone like her. You can bind her powers and make her the *least* powerful *kitsune* in the Chikara bloodline. I think that's the most condemning fate for scum like her."

While speaking with Esi, Darren hadn't noticed

Mack slip away. But of course it took someone with knowledge of Sakura's dark magic to free Fiona and her mother from their bonds. Mack playing the double agent had worked to their advantage yet again.

Ray was just telling Darren and Esi that he wasn't sure he knew enough yet to perform such a delicate curse when a familiar voice chimed in.

"You can do it, Ray!" Fiona said. "I know you can. I'll be your lucky charm."

"Fiona!" Darren called.

Hearing her voice, freed, felt like Christmas morning.

"I know you can too," Mack echoed.

Darren looked at Mack. This felt *better* than Christmas. Only Gabriella had spoken with Mack since he'd turned, and finally, Darren was looking at his friend again. His eyes got teary, and he quickly wiped them away and then clapped Mack on the back.

"We missed you, Mack," Darren said. "So much."

Mack nodded. He had missed them, too.

To help Ray out, Fiona sang the Amhrán Sinsear, this time without the dark verse, and stronger than she ever had before.

"That's the first time I was able to perform that song smoothly," Fiona said with a smile. "I think I had to really *mean* it, like Esi did with her forgiveness for Darren, and I do. I want to give you every bit of luck possible, Ray. You've got all of the Murphy clan on your side now."

"Thanks, I need it," Ray laughed. He asked Esi to tell him again what to do and which words to say.

Then there was another voice, this time from the outskirts of battle. It was Gabriella, who was still badly injured and couldn't move.

"You can do it, Ray," she yelled. "We beat Auden Ironbound in our first battle. Your power is strong. We know you can do this."

Ray nodded. It was on him now—and on Darren's smooth training.

Although she was outnumbered, Sakura moved into physical attack. Mr. Kimura's moves were swift—far more swift than anyone would have given the old man credit for. He moved quickly, matching her step for step, pounce for pounce.

Darren concentrated on bringing electricity to the tips of his fingers. The sparks came together, and he tried to throw a force field around Sakura. But magic was keeping her tied to Mr. Kimura. The field went up around the two of them.

Sakura didn't try to fight. She glanced at the group around her with a curious expression, as if the fact that they were working together and helping one another was amusing.

Finally, Ray drew electricity to his fingertips and began to chant the spell Esi taught him. This time, the magic worked. His sparks moved forward, binding Sakura's wrists with handcuffs. Then, when Ray said the correct words, the electricity moved into her body, rippling from within her.

Sakura howled with rage. She tried to raise some of her followers to come to her defense, but it was too late. She had no followers left—no able-bodied ones, anyway. While Darren and the others watched, her sleek black hair turned gray. Darren thought her *kitsune* pelt must have done the same.

Ray had done it.

The Shadow Fox's powers—and *only* the Shadow Fox's powers—were bound.

Mack, standing next to Darren, slumped to the ground. He could feel his heartbeat pulse in his wrists. It was over. The war was over.

"We did it," he whispered.

They had.

Chapter 13
CIRCE'S PROPHECY

There was total silence.

Slowly, the wounded Changers began to rise—Sakura's forces and the Changer nation alike. The *selkies* and the skinwalkers, too.

One old woman dropped to her knees in front of Fiona. "Forgive me, Your Royal Highness," she said.

Fiona touched the top of the woman's head. "I know you were only trying to protect the *selkies*," she said.

The *selkies* all turned to Fiona, Mack, Darren, and Gabriella and bowed. Then the remaining Changer groups rose and did the same.

What are they doing? Mack wondered, glancing around. *Are they bowing . . . to us?*

These were not the frightened bows that he had witnessed when Sakura was still in charge of her army. This energy was totally different. Sakura's forces bowed to her out of fear. These Changers were bowing out of love and respect.

Jiichan's face wrinkled into a broad smile.

The rest of the First Four—Yara, Sefu, and Ms. Therian—arrived on the battlefield a moment later to stand behind him. Mack flinched when he noticed that Ms. Therian's leg was in a protective cast, but she was smiling too, like nothing bothered her in the world. He had never seen the First Four so happy.

Mack wasn't sure what to do. "Should I bow too?" he asked. "What's everyone bowing for?"

"They're bowing to you—to the four of you," Yara said, including Darren, Fiona, and Gabriella with a wave of her hand. "They have accepted the prophecy that named you the next First Four."

Gabriella stifled a laugh. It was a solemn moment, but it was also confusing. "They accept us? What does that—what does that *mean*?"

"It means you are the youngest First Four to ever take power," Ms. Therian says. "You are the First Four now. Our work is done."

Mack watched Fiona's eyes widen. "But—but you're the First Four!" she stammered.

"Not anymore," Sefu said.

Jiichan cleared his throat. He spoke loud enough for everyone on the battlefield to hear. "Today, you four have shown the Changer nation what it needed most: encouragement. Leadership. Teamwork. Loyalty. Mercy. Without those qualities, we would not have won this battle."

He smiled at each of them. "Today, you have taken our reigns. You have shown us all what it is to be true leaders. And in doing so, you became the leaders of the Changer nation."

"How did we do that?" Mack asked. "Ray saved everyone. Not us."

"We all saw the way you helped one another, and the way you led Ray. You showed tremendous kindness and mercy—not just for our supporters but also for the dark forces against us. That's what the Changer nation needed to see," Mr. Kimura said.

"They've accepted Circe's prophecy. They can see that you are the new First Four," Ms. Therian said. "It's a very magical moment."

I need a few minutes to wrap my brain around this, Mack thought. *I'm not sure I'm ready.* He could see that Gabriella, Darren, and Fiona were having similar thoughts.

The Changers around them, however, were waiting for the new First Four to say something. Mack waited for one of the others to step up. Surely Fiona or Darren or Gabriella wanted to speak, but they only nodded at him.

I guess I have to be the one do this, Mack thought.

He cleared his throat and turned to address all the Changers in Central Park, thankful that their protections kept out any nonmagical folk.

"Whether you fought alongside us as friends, or against us as enemies, we've all got to come together," he said. "I know I can speak for the others when I say we will show mercy to anyone who wants to be part of the *peaceful* Changer nation."

Sakura's forces threw up a quiet cheer. Mack could almost see the dark magic that held them in its clutches dissipating.

"We can never again let one faction or a dark power get the better of us. That's not who we are. That's not what Circe wanted us to be. We're all Changers, all right? Let's come together."

Suddenly, Mack realized *why* he was always so uncomfortable with the idea of being called a member of the First Four. *The title's all wrong*, he thought. *It forces us to play a role we shouldn't play. A role that alienates and frightens some of the Changer factions. Factions of those who helped us—those like the* selkies.

"We may be the new First Four, but I think—I think we can go for a title change." He smiled at his friends. "I think we'll just be the Four Helpers. What do you guys think? We're here to help, but this is *your* Changer nation. We don't ever want anyone to lose sight of that again."

All the Changers began to cheer.

Leana pulled Fiona into a hug. "We have a long way to go," she said, looking at the Four Helpers. "But I think, with you four at the helm, we will finally have a nation that brings *everyone* together."

Mack smiled at her, feeling proud and confident. The

selkies had been separated from the rest of the Changer nation for a long time. For her to say what she did meant that they really could all come together.

Gabriella's wounds had been healed enough, and now she began to make the rounds with Daniel, the *nahual* who had first taught her about healing. Her *tía* Rosa and her grandmother did the same. Mack noticed that they were healing Sakura's former soldiers as well as their own. He shook his head. No, he thought. *It wasn't Sakura's forces versus them anymore. They were all one.*

Jiichan descended on Mack and enveloped his grandson in a hug.

"Can I ask something of you? Would you transform, Makoto?" Jiichan asked. "For too long I've only seen the shadowy form you took on when you joined Sakura—I want to see you as *you*, my grandson the Chikara, as the valiant *kitsune* you are."

Mack grinned.

"Anything for you, Jiichan," he said.

He transformed into his *kitsune* form. The beautiful white coat that had turned to an ashy gray when he joined Sakura was now white again. Mack looked down to admire himself, and that's when he saw it.

"A third tail," he said, transforming back. "I've earned a third tail."

"As I suspected," Mr. Kimura told him. "I wanted you to see that for yourself. I have every confidence that you will earn six more in your lifetime. Makoto—Mack. I am so very proud."

They embraced again.

———————

Back at home the four friends were in Mack's room, sharing a pizza. Ray was upstairs with the old First Four, figuring out his place in the Changer world. But to the four friends, it was almost like there was no care in the world. Comic books were strewn across the carpet— including one that Darren, Gabriella, and Fiona had created at Wyndemere Academy when Mack was still under Sakura's dark spell. They had missed him very much and hoped to give it to him someday.

"It's really great to have you back, Mack," Gabriella told Mack.

"We missed you," Fiona said quietly. "How do you feel?"

"I'm upset about my parents, I guess," Mack said. "But it's good to finally know the truth after all these years."

"It is," Fiona said. "Family secrets are always hard."

Of course Fiona would know.

They spent some time sitting there, laughing and talking. Gabriella nursed her leg, which was close to being fully healed, but not quite.

"So what's next for the Four Helpers?" Mack asked, grabbing a piece of pizza crust that Gabriella didn't want.

"Hopefully something *really* boring," Darren laughed. "Like math homework. Ooh, or an English paper!"

Gabriella sighed. "Are you *sure* there isn't another Shadow Fox, lurking somewhere?"

Everyone laughed.

After a few hours they all headed home. For the first time in a long time, they felt at peace. Of course, there would be other battles to fight. Other wars to wage. Other factions to unite.

But for tonight, even just for tonight, Mack was home with Jiichan, Darren and Ray were together,

Gabriella would have some hot chocolate with her sister, and Fiona could hug both of her parents at the same time.

And wasn't that what it was all about? Protecting the ones you love?

One thing was certain: whatever the four friends would face next, they'd face it together.

Bonus Chapter
A Changer Short Story

Esi Akosua flattened her skirt. She'd flattened her skirt maybe one hundred times that day. Esi was not a nervous girl, but today, she was nervous. Today, Esi was going to an important meeting with the new leaders of the Changer world.

It had been a few weeks since the Changer nation had fought off a dastardly *kitsune* named Sakura and her followers. Esi and her father were *anansi*—giant spiders—and had fought on the Changers' side. But not all of the *anansi* were willing to lie down and support the Changer nation. Her own grandmother, for example, was one of these people. Her grandmother believed that the *anansi* should fend for themselves and that the other types of Changers should do the same.

"It is tradition," the old woman had said.

"But sometimes traditions are meant to be broken," Esi had responded.

Her grandmother wouldn't relent.

The *anansi* were certainly stubborn, to say the least, which bothered Esi. She wanted everyone to get along. And that was why Esi had called this meeting in the first place—to find out what she could do.

So that was how Esi was about to eat dinner, alone, with the four new leaders of the Changer nation—Fiona, Darren, Gabriella, and Mack. Her father had offered to come, but she denied his request. If four middle school students from Willow Cove were the next leaders of the Changer nation, Esi was going to be the next middle school leader of the *anansi*.

Still, Esi's father was a cautious man. He'd flown her to Willow Cove—where the Changers lived—on his friend's private jet. She had then met a driver (another friend of her father's) who escorted her to Mack's house, where the Changers were based. Her father was protective, but Esi didn't blame him. She was the keeper of an important ancient relic. In the wrong hands, the relic could start a whole new Changer War.

Esi took a deep breath. Although she knew Fiona, Darren, Gabriella, and Mack, this was far more important than just meeting friends for dinner. She was representing the entire *anansi* faction. It was a weighty responsibility, and an important one.

Until very recently, Esi hadn't interacted with many other Changers, aside from other *anansi*. She trained with other *anansi*. She ate with other *anansi*. She played with other *anansi*. The *anansi* even had strict customs on what was proper and what was not. Her grandmother had seen to it that Esi knew them.

What would dinner with the Changers be like? Esi was about to find out.

Esi flattened her skirt one last time and knocked on the door of the house.

In *anansi* tradition, Esi would have to be invited inside, but this did not happen. Instead, she heard a girl's voice coming from within.

"It's Esi!" the girl said, peeking out the window. She

then directed her voice to Esi. "Just come on in. The door's unlocked!"

Esi took a deep breath. It felt wrong, not to shake out her shoes and enter when guided, but she pushed open the door anyway.

"Esi!" a chorus of voices yelled, and then the voices' owners ran over to hug her. There was Mack, a *kitsune*; Fiona, a *selkie*; Darren, the *impundulu*; his brother Ray, also an *impundulu*; and Gabriella, a *nahual*.

Each one of them wore comfy clothes, like jeans and a T-shirt or, in Gabriella's case, messy hair in a bun and sweatpants. Esi worried she was overdressed in her skirt and button-down top (thankfully, she hadn't worn heels), but if she was, no one said anything. Quite the opposite, actually—she felt warm and welcomed.

"Esi the best-y! It's good to see you in Willow Cove," Darren cheered with a big smile. He gestured toward the rest of the house. "This is our base, where Mack and his grandfather, Akira Kimura, live. We do almost all of our planning here—"

"And pizza eating," Mack cut him off.

"Which is equally as important," said Ray.

"If not more," said Gabriella.

"Definitely more," added Fiona.

They were all very in sync. Thankfully, it wasn't that intimidating kind of sync. Esi felt comfortable. More comfortable than she did at most *anansi* dinners, anyway.

"Dinner is just about ready. It's spaghetti and meatballs. Mr. Kimura wouldn't trust us to make anything else, so I hope that's okay," Darren told her. "*Someone* singed the burgers last time," he said, shooting a sharp look in Ray's direction.

"They weren't burned, they were *well done!*" Ray fought back, sparking a bit of lightning with his fingertips.

Esi laughed.

"Spaghetti and meatballs sounds delicious," she said. "It's a classic. Anyway, I'm starving. Let's eat!"

The six of them sat around Mack's kitchen table. Eating with these Changers was very different than eating with the *anansi*, Esi realized—it wasn't nearly as rigid. For example, Darren slurped his spaghetti. Fiona refilled the water pitcher with her *selkie* powers. Ray lit some candles with his lightning. And at one point, Mack and Gabriella raced each other to the kitchen for more spoons.

With the *anansi*, Esi always felt like she was being watched and evaluated. She felt like she was told to sit straighter, or eat faster, or talk slower. This dinner, though? This felt comfortable. This felt like home. She didn't feel like they were in a meeting or some other kind of formality. It was almost like . . . like she really was just there to be friends.

"So my little bro says you're the reason I'm an *impundulu* now," Ray said through a mouthful of noodles and cheese. "And to think I almost graduated college without majoring in Lightning Studies."

"You still haven't 'almost graduated,' though," Gabriella corrected him. "Those charred burgers last week set you back."

The entire table laughed.

"Yeah, our ancestors had some major issues with each other," Esi replied, bringing the subject back around. "I guess spaghetti and meatballs didn't exist back then, or they probably wouldn't have cursed each other."

"No spaghetti and meatballs? I probably would have cursed everyone too," Mack said.

"If only we'd thought of that while battling Sakura," Gabriella said. "Just feed her some spaghetti and meatballs, and she'd be a docile lamb. That would have saved us some time."

Mack shot her a playful look. "Tell me about it," he said.

Mack had spent the majority of the war as a double agent on her side.

"Jokes aside, we are really glad that you could join us for dinner today, Esi," Fiona said briskly. "As you know, I'm a *selkie*. The *selkies* and *anansi* are similar in some ways—we both come from factions that don't traditionally support the Changer nation, and I know how rough and stressful it can be."

"You're right," Esi agreed. "The *anansi* like to have our own way. But we are not united like the *selkies*. My father and I are willing to pledge ourselves to the greater good of the Changer nation, but it's going to be a hard battle convincing the rest. We don't have a queen like you do, for example, or a set leader."

Fiona seemed to understand.

"It can be hard, trying to please two groups at once, and knowing they are both right," she said.

Esi smiled. None of her other *anansi* friends seemed to grasp what it was like—to straddle two realms. She was glad to speak with someone who understood.

"*Anansi* like our tradition. My grandmother is a wonderful woman, but she's unwilling to come to the defense of strangers. If only she could *see*—"

"You mean, if only she could taste this delicious spaghetti and meatballs," Mack cut in.

Esi waved him off. "If only she could see other Changers, maybe she could understand that what we all want is really the same—to protect humans and uphold the peace, for each other."

Esi bit her lip. That was exactly what she'd wanted to say. How could they unite their two groups, and any other groups in the growing Changer nation?

The Four Helpers and Ray paused for a bit, thinking about the situation.

"It's a delicate situation," Gabriella admitted.

"A very delicate one," Darren added.

Then Fiona started rustling in her seat.

"Actually, I think I have an idea," she said. "Esi, you only train with other *anansi*, right?"

Esi nodded.

"That is correct," she said.

"The *selkies* only train with *selkies*, too. I'd never met another youngling *selkie* until I visited the isles, not even at Wyndemere Academy. But what *if*—what if we set up a system, kind of like a pen pal system, where members of the factions get to meet each other? I think a *selkie-anansi* team-up could be a lot of fun. Or *impundulu-anansi*. Since, you know, that ancient curse thing and all."

Esi's face brightened.

"Fiona, I think you're on to something!" she said. "It's a wonderful idea. If we can get people talking outside of their communities—"

"They'll be more open to hearing each other speak—" Fiona cut in.

"—and we'll be able to make some really cool connections!"

Esi beamed. It was a good plan. She suddenly felt

happier that she had chosen to have dinner with the Four Helpers.

Darren wiped some tomato sauce off his chin.

"Esi, would you be interested in helming that? The worldwide Changer pen pal system? We could use someone like you on our team, someone smart and really passionate about this."

Esi's cheeks flushed. "I would be honored," she said. "I will talk with the *anansi* and try to get them on board with the first step."

"And it will be more than the *anansi*, of course, but that's a great starting place," Fiona added. "I'd love to take you with me to meet the *selkies* at the water's edge. Maybe we could visit some of the Changer factions in western Europe and Southeast Asia, too. *The Compendium* has a complete list of Changer factions—we should go to each and every one."

It was so like Fiona to suggest looking in their book, *The Compendium*. Fiona knew that if there was something to be found, you could find it in a book.

"You'd basically be the public relations director of the Changers and the Changer nation," Gabriella said, arching her brow. "Which sounds daunting, but I think you can do it. You in, Esi?"

"Am I?" Esi laughed. "I mean, I guess I have to, since I *did* make Ray get his powers and all. . . ."

The table laughed.

"See, this is how we gotta lead," Mack told everyone. "It's a group effort. Otherwise things will get really sticky, and some factions will start to feel like they're left out. We don't want that."

"Speaking of feeling left out, I think you left something big out of this dinner, Mack," Ray said seriously.

Mack glanced around.

"Oh no," he mumbled. "Like what?"

Ray pointed a finger at his empty plate.

"Where's the dessert? Mmm, I could go for some *dorayaki* right about now."

"Did anybody say *dorayaki*?" Darren asked, coming out of the Kimura kitchen. He was holding a plate of *dorayaki*—Japanese pancakes with whipped cream—and they looked like the most delicious things that Esi had ever seen.

"Shall we make a toast?" Darren asked.

"With pancakes?" asked Esi.

"Fine, fine, we'll make a *pancake*," Gabriella said.

Esi laughed. "I suppose we shall," she said.

They raised their *dorayaki* and clinked them together.

"To the Changer nation!" they said.

"And pancakes!" Darren added.

"And pancakes," everyone chorused.

Esi couldn't wait.